COMANCH'

With white man's contempt, they called him Comanch', the Indian. He didn't know if they were right or not, and he'd have to keep tracking the shadow of his past till he found out. But—whether he was Indian, white man, or half-breed—no one would spit that name at him any more. The last man who called him Comanch' woke up in Doc Peter's Office. The next man who tried it might never wake up again . . .

Cliff Farrell was born in Zanesville, Ohio, where earlier Zane Grey had been born. Following graduation from high school Farrell became a newspaper reporter. Over the next decade he worked his way west by means of a string of newspaper jobs and for thirty-one years was employed, mostly as sports editor, for the *Los Angeles Examiner*. He would later claim that he began writing for pulp magazines because he grew bored with journalism. His first Western stories were written for *Cowboy Stories* in 1926 and his byline was A. Clifford Farrell. By 1928 this byline was abbreviated to Cliff Farrell, and this remained for the rest of his career. In 1933 Farrell was invited to contribute a story for the first issue of *Dime Western*. He soon became a regular contributor to this magazine and to *Star Western* as well. In fact, many months he would have a short novel in both magazines. Farrell became such a staple at Popular Publications that by the end of the 1930s he was contributing as much as 400,000 words a year to their various Western magazines. In all, Farrell wrote nearly 600 stories for the magazine market. His earliest Western fiction tended to stress action and gun play, but increasingly his stories began to focus on characters in historical situations and the problems faced by those characters. *Follow the New Grass* (1954) was Farrell's first Western novel, a story concerned with a desperate battle over grazing rights in the Cheyenne Indian reserve. It was followed by *West with the Missouri* (1955), an exciting story of riverboats, gamblers, and gunmen. *Fort Deception* (1960), *Ride the Wild Country* (1963), *The Renegade* (1970), and *The Devil's Playground* (1976) are among the best of Farrell's later Western novels. *Desperate Journey*, a first collection of Cliff Farrell's Western short stories, has also been published.

COMANCH'

Cliff Farrell

GUNSMOKE

First published in the UK by Ward, Lock

This hardback edition 2006
by BBC Audiobooks Ltd
by arrangement with
Golden West Literary Agency

ISBN 1 4056 8072 5

British Library Cataloguing in Publication Data available.

Printed and bound in Great Britain by
Antony Rowe Ltd., Chippenham, Wiltshire

CHAPTER ONE

Standing on the gallery of Casa Bonita, Mike Bastrop tossed a scatter of gold coins among the riders of his trail crew, and watched with amusement as they scrambled for the money.

They were saddle-hardened men, made savage by long-denied wants. They were ragged, with bellies wolf-lean after months on the drive to Kansas and return.

It took five days of riding to earn a five-dollar gold piece. Five dollars would buy whisky enough to drown a man's memories of the hardships, hire a woman's kisses for a night, blank out the fears of the future for a few hours at least.

They fought like wild dogs for the coins, cursing and sweating. It was the law of survival. The biggest and strongest among them came up with the major share of the booty.

"That's a little extra to blow in on the fandango gals," Mike Bastrop said. "But be mighty sure that such of you as I'm keeping on the payroll will be in shape to ride when you show up for work. I'll give you two days to have your fling. Then, we're shaping up a late drive and heading north again."

His eyes rested briefly on one of the riders. Lee Jackson was the only man who had not joined in the melee for the tossed coins. He had remained apart, watching the others maul each other in the struggle.

It had always been that way with Lee Jackson. He had ridden with them to Kansas, lined up with them at the chuckwagon for his meals, shared tobacco and canteen water with them when those items were in short supply. He had more than shared the work and the miseries.

Mike Bastrop, who acted as his own trail boss, had a habit of giving Lee Jackson the worst of it. Come a dry stretch where the dust hung in the blazing sun, it would be Lee Jackson who rode drag, breathing through a necker-chief as he prodded the laggards along.

More often than any other member of the crew, he drew the graveyard shift on which a man was awakened in his blankets two hours before daybreak to stand the last watch on the bed grounds until the herd was thrown on the trail. Then he rode swing or drag until dusk, sixteen to eighteen hours a day during the long June marches on the road to Kansas.

"Good enough for him," Mike Bastrop had said more than once. "The nerve of him, trying to palm himself off as the son of my poor, dead wife!"

There were other things Mike Bastrop said about Lee Jackson. "He's all Indian," Bastrop had declared repeatedly. "He looks like 'em. He thinks like 'em. He'll act like one, sooner or later. He's Comanch', I tell you."

Even Bastrop never said anything like that in Lee Jackson's presence, and he was not a man to spare the feelings of underlings. He was big, powerfully built, and in his forties. He was handsome in a hard-cut way, with a clipped black mustache and sideburns. He had appeared in the Punchbowl not long after Appomattox, wearing the tattered tunic of a Confederate major. He was said to have served under Jubal Early, but there were whispers that he had actually been one of Cantrell's guerrillas.

He now owned Rancho Verde. Its range stretched from the breaks of the Pecos River on the west to the dry plains beyond the Armadillo Hills, with the bluffs of the Staked Plains rising in the distance.

Comanch'! The last man who had used that term in Lee Jackson's hearing had revived in Dr. Obey Peters' office in Punchbowl. Lee Jackson's fists had dealt the damage.

"Next time, cowboy," Obey had said as he patched up the victim, "pick on somebody that don't turn into a buzz saw. You ought to have seen the last feller they carried in here after he'd called Lee Jackson a Comanch'. He was a worse sight than you."

However, no matter how many men Lee Jackson fought, nothing was changed. Behind his back they still had a term that, in their minds, was an epithet. Comanch'.

He walked to the corral, cut out a powerful blue roan, and cinched down his worn saddle. He owned the roan personally, and had left it at the ranch when he had headed for Kansas with the drive. The wrangler had brought his horse in from pasture that morning. It was fat and in need of work, but Lee had never seen it reach the end of its endurance.

He mounted to ride away. In the pocket of his weathered duck jacket were twelve gold eagles. One hundred and twenty dollars. His pay for the months he had spent shaping up two beef herds and helping drive them north from New Mexico.

Two gunny sacks lay on the big cedar table in the main room of Casa Bonita. They had been brought back from Kansas in the chuckwagon, with the crew armed and acting as outriders, while Mike Bastrop and Bill Tice rode in the wagon with buckshot guns across their knees.

Mike Bastrop could afford to toss away a few extra coins after paying off the trail hands, for the sacks contained more than a hundred thousand dollars, the proceeds from the sale of the herds at the shipping point on the Santa Fe Railroad.

"You there, Jackson!" Mike Bastrop called. "I want you back here tomorrow. Kinky Bob tells me he's fetched in a string of green ones off the range to be broke. There's no time to lose. We'll need horseflesh in a hurry, what with one more drive to shove up the line before snow flies."

Lee did not answer. He wheeled his horse to head up the trail to town. He was long-legged, lean-fibered, with thick black hair, skin burned the color of rawhide, and very dark eyes.

A big man, who had stood in the background, excluded from taking part in the scramble for the money, called out, "See you tomorrow, Jack-Lee!"

The speaker was the wrangler, a black man who had no other name than Kinky Bob. He was a former slave, and his job was handling young, unbroken horses at Rancho Verde. He was even better at that art than Lee Jackson, whom he always addressed as Jack-Lee. That meant that Kinky Bob was the best rider of bad horses in the Punchbowl. Some cowboys said he might be the best in the world.

Lee Jackson grinned at Kinky Bob and nodded. He and Kink always worked together with the greenies. Shaping up Rancho Verde livestock took muscle and guts. A twister who got by a season without breaking a leg or an arm considered himself ahead of the game.

Mike Bastrop, a man who did not spare humans when

it came to working cattle, had learned that it paid to have his riders mounted on strong, powerful horses that had been expertly broken and trained so that they would not stampede a herd on the bed ground or cause trouble at the branding fires. He bought the best Morgan stallions and would have nothing to do with the broomtails that ran wild on the Staked Plains or beyond the Pecos.

Still standing was Bastrop's offer of a thousand dollars for the return of a big Barb stud that he had imported from Spain three years previously at a cost of more than six thousand dollars. The stallion was pure white, a rarity in Barbs, and had come from the stable of a grandee. It had jumped a high corral fence a few days after its arrival at Rancho Verde and had vanished. There were rumors that a white stallion had been sighted occasionally beyond the Armadillo Hills, but the big reward had never been claimed.

Lee watched Bastrop join two men who had been waiting in the background. The trio vanished into the cool dimness of the main room. El Casa Bonita had been built when the range was ruled by old Mexico. The beautiful house. It was adobe-built, shaded by galleries and vines and ancient oaks, mesquite and cottonwood. Hayfields were ripe beyond the spread of buildings. Ample water glinted in irrigation ditches.

Bill Tice and Judge Amos Clebe held drinks in their hands. Bill Tice owned the prosperous BT outfit a dozen miles northeast toward the Armadillos. He pooled his beef-raising with that of Rancho Verde and always went up the trail with the drives, acting as Mike Bastrop's *segundo*, or second in command.

Amos Clebe presided over court in Punchbowl, which was the county seat. The judge also held the office of county clerk and recorder. He and Bill Tice were Mike Bastrop's poker and drinking companions. Their poker games sometimes lasted for days and the stakes were said to be very stiff.

The hot, late-afternoon sun beat down on Lee as he rode toward Punchbowl. As usual he rode alone. He never felt comfortable with men who didn't seem to feel comfortable around him. And that meant almost everyone except Kinky Bob.

They believed Mike Bastrop was right in saying that

Lee Jackson was a Comanche. There were strains of Spanish and white blood in some of the tribes that cropped out after generations. Throwbacks, handsome and proud like this one. But Comanch', nevertheless. There was scarcely a person in the Punchbowl who had not lost a mother, a father, or other close kin to the lances and hatchets of raiding Comanches in the past.

The Comanches were now on reservation. They had not come down from the plains to raid and terrorize in more than a dozen years, but the memories remained. And the bitterness. Above all, the bitterness.

It had been some eighteen years ago when Lee had been brought to Rancho Verde by a cavalry sergeant and an Army scout who acted as interpreter. They had come from Fort Gilman, nearly two hundred miles away.

Lee had been about six years old. Instead of the breech-clout to which he was accustomed, he was clad in smothering homespun breeches and shirt that the wives of Army officers had forced upon him.

He spoke only the Comanche tongue, but from the facial expressions, he followed the gist of the conversation and any missing segments were explained to him later by the scout.

Mike Bastrop had stood on the same gallery from which he had tossed the coins, inspecting the ragged child with distaste. "What's this, sergeant?" he had demanded.

"A scoutin' detail come across this young one, alone an' runnin' for his life up north on the plains a few weeks ago," the soldier explained. "He was being chased by three Comanche warriors. They turned back when they saw the troopers. He told the interpreter he was the son of Quin-a-se-i-co. That's old Eagle-in-the-Sky, the big blue devil of the Comanche Nation. The boy seems to hate the chief, an' wanted to get away from Eagle's village."

"What's this got to do with me?" Bastrop demanded.

"The records show that this ranch was hit by the Comanches about four years ago," the sergeant explained. "Your wife, the former Señora Margarita Calvin, was killed along with three other adults, who were all that were at the ranch that day. You were in town on business, Major Bastrop. There was also a boy, less than two years old, whose remains were never found. There was the chance he had been taken with them by the Comanches. He was the Señora's son. Your stepson. He was named after his father, John Calvin, who was killed in the last few months of the war, fightin' for the reb—beggin' your pardon, sir—for the Confederacy. Colonel Graham thinks this boy might be your stepson."

"Ridiculous!" Mike Bastrop snorted. "This brat is Comanch'! You can see that for yourself."

Mike Bastrop grasped Lee by the hair, jerked his head back. "Why, he's not even a breed, by the looks. He's all Injun. You don't think I'm going to let the Army palm off a murderin' Comanch' whelp on me as my stepson, do you? This one, when he got old enough, would murder us in our beds."

"The Colonel thought it was worth a try," the sergeant admitted.

Mike Bastrop laughed. "I figured it that way. Your Colonel thought this would be an easy way to get an Indian off his hands."

"I wouldn't know anything about that, sir," the sergeant said with a smirk.

Mike Bastrop scornfully shook Lee by the hair. "What's your name, Injun?" he demanded.

Lee only glared at him, afraid, but defiant. He did not like this man.

"He doesn't seem to know even his own name," the sergeant said.

"My poor wife's son is dead," Bastrop said. "He was killed the same day Margarita was murdered by those red devils. I'll never stop mourning the fact that I happened to be away from the ranch that day. Otherwise I might have saved her and the child. Or, at least, have died with them."

Bastrop added, "But, in memory of Margarita, I'll look after this boy, at least long enough to give you fellows a chance to find his people—if he really has any white blood, which I doubt. He looks like he could stand a few square meals."

The Army had been only too happy to settle the problem in that manner. Lee had been made a ward of Mike Bastrop and had been placed in the hands of stern-minded Mexican women who helped with the kitchen and housework at Casa Bonita. They did not like Comanches, either. They treated him as an inferior and gave him the most menial tasks to perform.

"I'll give you a name," Mike Bastrop had told him. "After two of the greatest men that ever lived. I don't reckon an Injun ever heard of General Robert E. Lee or General Stonewall Jackson. But it might give even an Injun luck to be named after them. From now on, you're Lee Jackson. Don't ever try to make out that you're any kin of mine, or of my dead wife. I'll feed you and look after you, but I reckon you'll go back to the Comanches at first chance. Once an Injun, always an Injun."

Mike Bastrop had been wrong. Lee hadn't gone back to Indian life. He remembered the cruelty and hardships he had suffered at the hands of the Comanche chief and his squaws. He had tried twice previously to escape from Eagle's village. On both occasions he had been overtaken and carried back to Eagle-in-the-Sky's lodge.

Between the chief and the nameless youngster had been a deep, puzzling animosity. On Lee's part it had been a feeling that Eagle had committed an unforgivable wrong, but the exact nature of the act always escaped him.

In return, Eagle held toward him an emotion that was even greater than aversion. Fear, perhaps. But why would the great Quin-a-se-i-co, the Eagle chief of the Comanches, fear his own son, a mere boy?

Lee's determination to escape had never been quenched by his failures and the punishments Eagle had inflicted on him when he had been brought back. He wanted only to get away from Eagle and the silent *something* that lay between them. In his young mind had been only the intention of joining some other Comanche village where life might be easier. He had held no thought that he was other than a Comanche until the Army had brought up the question.

Each time he had made his bid to free himself from Eagle's cruelty he had struck southwesterly across the Staked Plains. It had seemed to him there was a tribe in that direction, or a haven, where he might find peace. A place where he belonged.

From the moment of his first meeting with Mike Bastrop he had made up his mind to flee from Rancho Verde and continue his attempt to find the Comanche village that was his imaginary place of safety.

For reasons he had never understood, he had kept putting off his departure. He grew to manhood and became a full-fledged vaquero. He still did not understand why he had not gone back to the Comanches. That was where he belonged. He had never been accepted here. The war trail was no more, but there were still remnants of the buffalo herds in the breaks of the plains. The Comanche spearmen would ride as long as meat was needed. He could be a spearman also. He would be accepted there. It was only Eagle-in-the-Sky who had persecuted him.

He rode now to town with white men's money in his pocket. Money was for spending. All he wanted was the sting of whisky in his throat, to drink until there were no memories in his mind, to forget the bitterness, to forget the ambitions he secretly held in his mind.

He stabled the roan at Ed Moorehead's livery. He rented a box stall and bought two measures of bran, ears of flint corn, and straw for bedding.

"You-all must purely think a heap o' that roan," the hostler said. "Spendin' almost a whole dollah on a hawss."

"Here's two bits more to see that he's pampered tomorrow in case I'm detained," Lee said.

The hostler hesitated. Lee had seen that expression in the faces of other men. Many times. Sam Barker, who was a bleary derelict, still had pride enough to feel ashamed of taking a gift from an Indian.

Lee pocketed the quarter. "Don't ever look at me like that again," he said.

He walked away. At the entrance to the wagon tunnel a high-stepping bay mare with a young woman in the side-saddle came racing into the barn at a gallop. He leaped aside to avoid being hit by the horse, but went sprawling in the dust. He looked up to see the disdainful delight in Clemmy O'Neil's gray-green eyes. She pulled the mare to a halt inside the barn, slid to the ground, and tossed the reins to the hostler.

"The mare will need a rub after she's cooled," she said. "I'm going back to the ranch tonight."

She removed her spurs and hung them on the saddle. She wore a gray riding habit and a straw sombrero held on her head by a chin strap. She pulled off the sombrero and arranged her unruly mop of red-gold hair.

Lee got to his feet and began whisking dust from his

breeches. Their eyes met briefly. Then Clemmy O'Neil turned away, offering no apology.

Lee walked out of the barn and headed down Sumner Street. He heard the crisp tap of the heels of Clementina O'Neil's riding boots a few paces back of him. He found himself walking faster. Nettled, he slowed to his former pace. She was trying to hurrah him. He wasn't in any hurry, and damned if he was going to let a vixen like Clemmy O'Neil prod him into dancing to her tune. She was always going out of her way to snub him and try to set herself a peg above him in the scale by which Punchbowl rated its people.

The peg for both of them was very low. That was one thing, at least, they had in common. She overtook him and walked past with a swish of her riding skirt. She had a figure and knew it. She was slim, and taller than average, with a healthy crop of freckles above a small nose in a very comely face. She always seemed to have a chip on her shoulder.

Lee saw the eyes of men along the street swing to watch Clemmy O'Neil as she walked past. She turned into Lucy Miller's sewing store. Now that she was out of sight the male onlookers began making remarks to each other. Their faces bore smirks.

Lee felt pity for Clemmy O'Neil—an emotion that would have touched off her short-fuse temper if she had known. He knew she would resent pity from anyone, most of all from a Comanche.

He walked into the Silver Bell. Combined music hall, gambling house, and saloon, it was a sizable establishment, the biggest between Denver and El Paso. Girls in bangles and beads were already on duty at this early evening hour, for everybody in Punchbowl knew that Mike Bastrop and Bill Tice had paid off their riders, and the crews would soon be hitting town with money to spend.

Lee moved to the bar. "Whisky," he said. "A bottle. The best you've got."

He saw in the bartender's eyes something of the same question the livery hostler's face had held. Every bar carried an Injun list, as it was called. Alcoholics, deadbeats, and squaw men were on the list. No liquor was to be sold to them. It was against the law to sell alcohol to an Indian.

Lee rarely had entered the Silver Bell in the past, for he knew he was not welcome there. He had made a point of appearing at its bar on occasion, but had never ordered more than a glass of beer. He knew his name was not officially on the Injun list. There apparently was still some doubt in the minds of some of the citizens of Punchbowl, at least, in spite of Mike Bastrop's attitude.

The bartender decided it was not up to him to make an issue of it. He wanted no trouble with the lean, dark rider with the burning challenge in his eyes. He produced a bottle. Lee paid for it and carried it to a table and sat down.

A percentage girl came sidling up. He looked at her and said, "What's your name, sweetheart? Susie?"

"Why, sure," she simpered. "Susie's a good name."

"I've met you before," Lee said. "In other places."

The liquor was fire and thunder. It eased the hurts, dulled the memories of cold rain and harsh wind and bitter nights on the trail. But that was all. It did not answer the questions he had asked himself all these years of growing up.

The arms of Susie were soft, clinging. Money was to spend. He spent it. It was only metal with which to buy forgetfulness and the company of these Susies of the world.

He drank again. And again. But the memories stayed with him. He gave Susie a gold piece. "Good-by, Susie!" he said. "Go away. That's for your own good. You don't want to be put on the Injun list do you?"

"Injun list?"

Lee laughed at her. She suddenly backed away from him. She was a stranger in Punchbowl. She hadn't known who he was.

He left the Silver Bell. Tomorrow he would be back where he belonged. At Rancho Verde, breaking wild horses with Kinky Bob. Having his guts jolted into his throat, his lungs hammered by the antics of an animal until blood showed on his lips.

He had drunk far more than he had ever drunk before. He had failed in his purpose. He had failed to erase the bitterness. He was not a part of the conviviality that was increasing in the town, for the crews were now pouring in, not only from BT and Rancho Verde, but from other outfits. But he was not one of them.

CHAPTER TWO

Four riders came down Sumner Street, pulled up in a flurry of hoofs, and swung down at a saloon ahead. They were from Bill Tice's BT outfit.

Bill Tice's two sons were in the group that came onto the sidewalk in Lee's path, stamping the kinks out of their legs after their ride.

Merl Tice recognized Lee. "How!" he said, lifting a palm in the peace sign. It was a common form of greeting among friends, meant to be humorous. It wasn't humorous the way Merl Tice said it.

The brothers hadn't gone up the trail with the drives in the spring, staying home to oversee the ranch. Lee had worked cattle with them in the past and had gone up the trail with them the previous year. There had never been any real trouble with them on his part. Neither had they become friends.

Merl, a couple of years older than Gabe, was the one who set the pattern for their thinking. The brothers were prototypes of their father—bony, lantern-jawed, and boisterous. The Tice ranch was making money, big money, and the Tices were the kind who believed that money gave them the right to ride roughshod over less fortunate neighbors.

There had been a time, so Lee had been told by older men, when the Tice ranch had been a starving, patched-saddle outfit in the coulees and dry benches along the toe of the Armadillos, with Bill Tice suspected of riding with a long loop on moonlit nights and with a running iron hidden in his boot.

That day was past. Bill Tice was now in virtual partnership with Mike Bastrop's mighty Rancho Verde. The Tices rode expensive saddles and owned race horses and wore handmade shirts with big pearl buttons, foxed breeches, and smoke-gray sombreros that cost fifty dollars a throw.

Gabe Tice, taking the cue from his brother, moved into Lee's path. Lee did not swerve. He shouldered Gabe aside and continued on down the sidewalk. Gabe took a stride to overtake him.

"Who'n blazes do you think you're pushin' around, you lousy In—!" he began.

His brother halted him. "Don't spoil a big evenin' by barkin' your knuckles on Lee Jackson," Merl Tice said. "He's drunk. Drunker'n a skunk."

Gabe subsided. "It's about time they quit sellin' whisky to some folks in these parts," he said. "There's a law ag'in it an' it ought to be heeded."

Lee's stride slowed. Then he kept going. He heard another word from the group. Comanch'!

The four men walked into the saloon. Which of them had uttered the word, Lee didn't know. It didn't matter. Either of the Tice brothers would be a handful in a fight. The chances were that he'd have all four of them on him if he took up the issue.

The whisky was having its effect. He wanted to stand in the middle of the street, lift a war whoop, and dare them to make the most of it. If he was Comanche, he was proud of it. The Spearmen were a proud race of warriors, marred only by the evil that was in Eagle-in-the-Sky.

He swallowed his anger. A sooty lantern burned in the tunnel in the livery stable. Sam Barker was playing solitaire in the lamplit cubby that served as an office. The hostler poked his head out of the door, scowled when he saw that it was Lee, and went back to his game.

Lee was fuzzy-headed as he began rigging the roan. He heard a new arrival enter the livery. "You can get out my mare for me," Clemmy O'Neil's voice spoke.

The hostler yawned and continued to riffle the cards. Lee remained out of sight in the box stall.

"Please hurry!" Clemmy O'Neil said.

"What's all the rush?" the man drawled. "Why go home so early? Ain't you missin' all the fun? All the boys are in town from the outfits tonight. Maybe you ought to stop in at the Silver Bell."

"Get my saddle on that mare as fast as you can!" Clemmy O'Neil's voice was shaking with humiliation.

The hostler laughed. "There was a time when the Bell got a bigger play on nights like this than all the other traps put together. They flocked to see Rose O'Neil like bears around spilled honey."

Clemmy O'Neil ignored that, waiting as the hostler slowly saddled her mount.

"All right," she finally exploded. "You can go back to your rat hole. Charge the fee to the BT account."

"Come on, dearie," the hostler said. "I'll lift you onto the saddle. It'll be a pleasure."

"You touch me with your filthy hands and I'll take a quirt to you," Clemmy O'Neil said.

"Suit yourself," the man said. "Maybe you'll change your tune. That mare's mighty skittish. She ain't in the mood to be rode home tonight, if you ask me. There's a stallion in the corral outside an' the mare knows it. You'll need luck, climbin' into that sidewheel hull. Just call me when you need me. An' say pretty please when you do."

The hostler was right. The girl had her hands full. Lee peered out. The mare was wheeling, pulling away, each time the girl tried to mount. She was dragged to her knees in the dust. She hung to the reins.

The hostler laughed again. "Say pretty please."

"Merl and Gabe will beat you to jelly if I tell them how you're acting," the girl gasped.

The hostler's amusement ended and he retreated hastily out of sight into his cubby.

Lee watched the struggle continue between the girl and the mare. She was weakening and was faced with the choice of releasing the reins or risk being trampled.

Lee had made up his mind not to interfere. Clemmy O'Neil had never treated him as anything better than the dust that was marring her garb. If anything, she had been even more disdainful of him than the majority.

Maybe that was because, like himself, she was listed on the lower end of the social scale in the Punchbowl. Women made a show of drawing aside the hems of their skirts when she passed by. Their husbands pretended that same brand of superiority, but only when their wives were around. Whenever they encountered Clemmy O'Neil alone, they eyed her with a different expression.

She was the daughter of Rose O'Neil, who had been the toast of the music halls from Denver to El Paso. Rose O'Neil was said to have had a fortune showered at her feet during the half-dozen years she had been known as the Golden Nightingale of the frontier towns. It was legend that she had squandered the money on clothes and jewelry as fast as it came into her hands. She had lived life to the full and had died tragically.

Ballads were still sung in line camps and around chuck-wagon fires:

> . . . lay still an' dead
> There on that silent stage.
> Lay dead there
> In ol' Punchbowl town,
> Our beautiful Rose O'Neil.

Rose O'Neil had been killed by a stray bullet while she was singing on the stage at the Silver Bell when a gunfight broke out among drunken cowboys. The man accused of firing the wild shot was lynched by a mob, but Rose O'Neil "lay still an' dead there on the silent stage."

When her will came to light it was learned she had a six-year-old daughter who was being raised in a convent in Santa Fe. As a young woman, Rose Shannon had been a seamstress and choir singer in Punchbowl, the daughter of a hard-working freighter. Against all advice, she had married a handsome, reckless Virginian named Clement O'Neil, who speculated in cattle and cotton and raced fast horses. He was killed in a horse race only a few months after their marriage, when his mount fell.

After the death of her husband, Rose O'Neil vanished for a time, then reappeared as a music-hall entertainer. Because of the beauty of her voice, men rode hundreds of miles to see and hear the Golden Nightingale.

Her will contained other surprises. It developed that Rose O'Neil's only other living relative was Bill Tice, owner of the BT outfit. The relationship was not of blood. Bill Tice had married Rose O'Neil's older sister when he was a young man. The sister had died a year or so after the marriage. Bill Tice had married again and Merl and Gabe were products of the second union.

As the only legal relative, Bill Tice was named guardian of the six-year-old Clementina O'Neil. It was understood that the Golden Nightingale had died almost penniless, but Bill Tice had made it known that he was a generous man who would see to it that his ward always had a roof over her head and a Christian upbringing, no matter how wild the blood that ran in her.

Therefore, Lee had not been the only one regarded as

outside the social pale in the Punchbowl. Clemmy O'Neil carried the same burden. And with the same refusal to acknowledge that any living being was better. Or to let anyone say a word against her mother in her presence without regretting the error.

Clemmy O'Neil was losing the battle with the mare. She was blinded by dust and in tears. She was being dragged around like a doll. She wasn't quitting, but her strength wasn't equal to the demand of her will. The reins slipped away. The mare started to bolt from the barn.

Lee emerged from the stall, caught the reins, dug in his heels, and brought the animal to a halt. "All right," he said. "Easy now. Easy, I say."

The animal began to calm. Clemmy O'Neil got to her feet, panting and quivering, and brushed her skirt.

"After you get your breath, I'll give you a hand up," Lee said. "She won't try to unload you. If she starts thinking of getting rank again, lay a quirt on her. Hard! Let her know you mean business."

Clemmy O'Neil approached. She was still breathing hard and was trembling. When Lee offered her a hand to assist her to mount, she straightened. The spitfire pride had returned.

"I need no help," she said. "Please stand aside."

The liquor was boiling in Lee. He was as angry as he had ever been in his life. To be scorned by the likes of Clemmy O'Neil.

"What you mean," he said, "is that you don't want to be touched by an Indian. Now, aren't you the proud one!"

She was near. Too near. She with her green eyes that held such scorn. Don't touch me, you outcast, she was telling him with her eyes.

He caught her in his free arm, pulled her against him, and kissed her on the mouth. It was done before she realized what was coming, before even he knew what he was doing. It was the whisky, perhaps. It was life, perhaps. It was his answer to Clemmy O'Neil's scorn, and to all the world.

She tore free. She snatched the quirt from her saddle and raised it to lay the lash across his face. Then she paused.

"You're drunk!" she cried. "Drunk!"

She pulled herself aboard the sidesaddle, fury giving her

strength. She struck the mare with spurs and rode out of the barn. Lee heard the hoofbeats fade down Sumner Street.

He saw Sam Barker's leering face peeking out of the cubby. The man had seen him forcibly kiss Clemmy O'Neil. He turned unsteadily away. What did it matter? He made his way to his horse, pulled himself into the saddle, and rode out of the barn.

His thoughts were addled. Time seemed to be slowed so that impulses passed sluggishly across his mind. The truth was that he had never been drunk before. He had seen drunken men sing and dance. He wondered why he did not feel like singing or dancing. He had seen others weep in their cups. He did not feel like weeping. He only felt empty. And alone.

He ran his hand over his lips. His lips which had touched the lips of Clementina O'Neil. He regretted what he had done. He had treated her in the way most men wanted to treat her—as the daughter of the flaming Rose O'Neil.

He felt deep pity for Clemmy O'Neil, an attitude that he knew she would resent bitterly. She would want pity from no one, least of all Lee Jackson.

He found himself standing at the bar of the worst dive in town. He was drinking whisky he didn't remember ordering and it was bitter in his throat. What he sought was oblivion. From everything. From all memories, and especially from the thought that he had added to Clemmy O'Neil's burden.

He fumbled for his watch. It was a cheap, nickel-plated piece with a buffalo-tooth fob that he had bought from a peddler on the trail to Kansas. It was missing from his pocket.

The banjo clock on the saloon wall said ten o'clock. He left the place, mounted his roan, and headed down the trail toward Rancho Verde. That was all he remembered. After that came oblivion that had been eluding him all evening.

Dawn was in the sky when he awakened, stiff, cold, and forlorn, with a throat as dry as alkali. His horse was nuzzling for forage nearby, its reins dragging. He had slept in high grass near a shallow stream.

He identified his location. Soldier Ford. Casa Bonita

was still five miles south. The trail forded the creek nearby, but he and his horse had been hidden by brush and darkness from any travelers who might have passed by during the night.

He drank from the stream. And drank again. He buried his face in the cooling water. He reached for his watch. When he failed to find it, he recalled that it had been missing before he had left town. He decided that he must have dropped it in the livery barn.

He had slept here five or six hours. A period of total oblivion. That realization now appalled him.

He mounted and rode to Rancho Verde. Full daylight had come, but lamps still burned back of the curtains in Casa Bonita. Judge Amos Clebe's varnished buggy stood, shafts hoisted, alongside the house. Bill Tice's silver-trimmed saddle was stored on a tree on the gallery of the house. The poker game was still on.

The bunkhouse stood a considerable distance west of the main house. It was dark and deserted, for all hands were still in town. Only a few line riders at lonely shacks out in the range were on duty.

Kinky Bob appeared. He lived alone in a low, dirt-roofed adobe shack near the barn and wagon shed. His home had once been the quarters of a slave family. He had just cooked and finished his breakfast and had a tin cup of coffee in his hand.

Lee dismounted, drew his rig from the roan, turned it into the corral, and saw that it had water and feed. Kinky Bob came closer, took a long look at him, then whistled and hurried back to his shack.

He returned with another tin of black coffee. "You sure look like you need it, Jack-Lee," he said.

The coffee helped a little. "There's a woodpecker hammering on my skull," Lee sighed. "And danged if I can scare him away."

"You look like you're goin' to enjoy bronc twistin' a lot less than usual," Kinky Bob said.

Lee groaned. "My head's going to sail right off into the tules the first time a horse sunfishes on me today. And good riddance."

"You git any sleep atall, Jack-Lee?"

"I woke up in the brush at Soldier Ford. I must have snored there for hours. You ever been drunk, Kink?"

"I ain't sayin'. But I know you'll be all right. You young. You come back in a hurry. Wait 'til yo're old. Like Kinky Bob. Older'n sin. I kin hear my bones creak every time a snuffy horse humps his back under me."

Lee grinned weakly. He had no idea how old Kink really was. Nor did Kink. Frost was in his tough, curly hair, but to Lee he was a powerful rock that would never change. In his youth he had been trained as a boxer. No man had ever defeated him.

Lee ate the flapjacks and grits Kink cooked for him. They saddled up, each picking as his mount his smartest cutting horse, trained for assisting with green animals. They loaded a pack animal with food and bedrolls.

The poker game evidently was still going on in Casa Bonita. The wan light of lamps continued to burn back of the velvet curtains even though sunup was at hand.

At this hour the air was keen and bracing. It drove the last of the murk from Lee's thoughts. They rode in silence for a time, heading westward for the horse pasture two miles away where there were pole corrals and squeezers to help with handling rough horses.

"Why'd you do it, Jack-Lee?" Kinky Bob finally asked.

Lee didn't bother trying to evade. He knew what Kink meant. "I guess things just got to closing in on me a little too snug," he said.

"Such as de boss orderin' you out to bust horses the very next day after you got back from de long trail?"

"Maybe," Lee replied.

"Seems like, bein' as he tuk you to raise, he don't show much mercy to you."

Lee looked at the big man. Kinky Bob met his gaze. "He hate you, Jack-Lee."

"I've never done anything to him, Kink."

"Comanches, dey kill de lady dat was his wife as she sat right in dat house, so I was told. Dey tried to burn de house itself, but de walls an' big beams was too old an' tough. De Majah, he remember who done dem things."

Lee was silent for a time. "I see your point. Mike Bastrop has reason to hate Comanches. But he took me in and raised me. Why? He could have sent me to an orphanage."

"Or had you sent back to Eagle-in-the-Sky," Kinky Bob said. "He tried to do dat."

"Back to Eagle?" Lee exclaimed. "What are you saying?"

"De Majah, he made a trip to Fo't Gilman not long after you was first brung here when you was a button. He tried to talk de Colonel into sendin' you back to de chief. He said Eagle was yore father. Said you was Injun an' you belonged with yore people."

Lee peered at the big man. "How do you know this?"

"I was breakin' hawsses for de Army at de fo't when he come dar. De Colonel's orderly tol' me all about it. I didn't pay much 'tention at de time. I didn't come here to Rancho Verde 'til a few years afterward to work for dat man. Since den I been doin' a lot of seein'. An' thinkin about you."

"What did the Colonel say?"

"Said he wasn't convinced that you was a Comanch'. He said he'd have you put in an orphanage somewhere. Majah Bastrop changed his tune. Said he'd look after you 'til you was big enough to fend for yourself. De Colonel was happy to let it stand dat way."

Kinky Bob was silent for a time. "Why don't you pull out, Jack-Lee?" he finally asked. "Change yore name. Go somewhere else. Forgit de Punchbowl. Forgit de Majah. He give you all de tough jobs. Everybody know dat. It's like he wants to make you pay for what happened to de lady."

Lee rode for minutes without speaking. "What you're advising me to do, Kink," he finally said, "is go somewhere, change my identity, and never let anyone know I'm a Comanche."

"I didn't say dat, Jack-Lee."

"You believe I *am* a Comanche, don't you, Kink?"

"Kink don't believe nothin'," the big man exclaimed.

"I'm not pulling out," Lee said. "At least not yet. I don't savvy why I hang on. I've decided to leave. A hundred times. But something keeps holding me here."

CHAPTER THREE

They reached the fenced pasture where the new crop of unbroken horses was held. The animals were all five-year-olds that had been cut from the main herd and brought off the range for training.

Lee and Kinky Bob began their task. Working animals in groups of half a dozen, they sought, first of all, to win their confidence by moving among them, accustoming them to the presence of humans. Next would come the critical period of letting them smell saddle blankets and of submitting to the feel of a halter.

It was a tough day's work, with animals rearing and striking with lightning hoofs. Patience and more patience. Try and try again. Dust and blistering sun. Gain an inch, lose an inch. Start over. Talk gently, confidently. Beware of the slash of savage teeth. Teeth that did not always miss.

They quit at sundown. Bone-weary, they had a respectable string of horses submitting to the weight of a saddle blanket, and a few even accepting a halter.

They stripped and reveled in the cool water of the irrigation ditch. They washed their dust-caked garments, hung them to dry on brush, and donned clean replacements.

They had set up camp in the horse pasture in order to accustom the animals to the presence of humans and to the smells and sounds of a cookfire. It developed they had failed to include salt in their food pack. Kinky Bob saddled up and headed for his shack to fetch the essential condiment.

Lee, with half an hour to wait, rolled another cigaret, opened a can of tomatoes, and tested the contents. It was without zest, lacking salt. He went to the ditch, scoured the Dutch oven with sand and water in order to pass time.

He straightened. Riders were approaching. Several riders. The sun had gone down and the range was sinking into a sea of purple mist. The riders who loomed out of the dusk were miraged to the stature of giants on mighty horses. But they were mere men.

There were five of them. Mike Bastrop was the nucleus of the contingent. With him were his poker-playing cronies, Bill Tice and the pudgy, gray-bearded jurist, Amos Clebe. For once, the fastidious Judge was riding saddleback, rather than in his gleaming top buggy which was more suited to his paunchy, soft physique.

The other two were Bill Tice's sons. Merl and Gabe Tice held Lee's attention as they dismounted. They had the attitude of avengers on the prowl. They bore the flinty glare of pursuers who had overtaken their quarry.

Bill Tice also dismounted, but Mike Bastrop and the Judge remained in the saddle. All five were armed with pistols. Rifles jutted from slings on the saddles of the Tice brothers.

Kinky Bob loomed up in the background and halted his horse. Evidently he had turned back when he had met the five on their way to the pasture. His face was ashine with uneasiness.

"All right," Mike Bastrop said. "There he is, men. It's your pleasure."

Lee, astounded, stood staring. Merl and Gabe Tice came walking toward him. Not until too late did he comprehend that they meant harm. However, they made no move to draw their pistols. His own .44 and his rifle were out of reach.

Merl snarled, "You filthy copperpot, if you live a million years, you'll never quit bein' sorry you tried to lay a hand on our kind of women."

Merl and Gabe came at him from left and right. Lee, still stunned by the suddenness of it, only partly warded off the first fist that came at him. Gabe seized his arm and whirled him off balance. He was exposed to the smashing blow that Merl drove at his jaw, staggering him.

He braced his heels and pivoted. Gabe was many pounds heavier, but Lee lifted him clear of the ground and whip-cracked him, sending him slithering into the fringe of the fire.

Gabe uttered a grunt of fear, but rolled clear, brushing away sparks, without serious damage. Lee ducked, twisting aside, for he sensed that Merl was coming at him from the opposite side. He felt Merl's arms slide over his head, failing in an attempt to pin his arms to his sides.

The brothers circled him. He moved in on Merl and rammed a fist to the stomach. Merl reeled back with a wheeze of agony.

Bill Tice now came to the aid of his sons. He leaped on Lee's back. He was a powerful man, and Lee, his lungs already burning from the stress of the battle, was unable to shake him off.

Gabe moved in, fists poised. "Wait a minute!" Lee panted. "What's come over you people? What's this all about?"

Mike Bastrop spoke. "You know what you did, you whelp. You ought to be hung. Tie him to that mesquite snag over there, boys. Use my quirt if you want."

Kinky Bob spoke in his deep voice. "You ain't goin' to horsewhip him? Not dat!"

Bastrop whirled on the black man. "What have you got to say about it? Maybe you'd like a taste of a quirt, too. We don't stand for white men trying to break into the sleeping rooms of our women, let alone an Indian."

"What are you talking about?" Lee demanded.

Merl Tice slapped him savagely. "You know," he raged. "You insulted my sister last night at the livery, then followed her to the ranch, knowin' she'd be alone. You tried to bust in on her."

Lee quit struggling to escape from Bill Tice's arms. "Your sister? You mean Clemmy O'Neil? No! No! I couldn't do a thing like that!"

Merl slapped him again. "You grabbed her ag'in her will at the livery! Don't deny that. Sam Barker saw it. You followed her out of town."

Ice suddenly rushed through Lee's veins. He was thinking of those hours of blankness the previous night. Had he really lain asleep in the brush at Soldier Creek all that time? The Tice ranch house was little more than an hour's ride from the ford.

They saw the uncertainty in him. Merl struck him again. He felt blood flow from a split lip.

"All I ask is that I get first whack at him with the quirt," Merl gritted. "We ought to drag him by the heels back to the BT so that Clemmy can see him pay for scarin' her out of her wits."

"You mean she says I was there?" Lee demanded. "She saw me?"

"O' course she saw you. You ain't goin' to add to your troubles by callin' my sister a liar, are you?"

His father spoke wrathfully. "She ain't your sister, Merl, an' I don't want you claimin' the likes of her as such. But, even so, she's a woman an' is entitled to protection from the likes of this one."

"She's lying," Lee said, and suddenly he was sure of it. "She couldn't have seen me at BT last night. I wasn't within miles of your ranch."

"Then how do you explain why this was found in her room after she fought you off?" Merl demanded.

He dangled an object in front of Lee's eyes. It was the pocket watch with the buffalo-tooth fob that had been missing from Lee's pocket. He could only gaze at it, bewildered.

Amos Clebe said, "I reckon there wasn't any real harm done to the gal. I say to give this fellow a hiding, then run him out of the country. As a legally elected representative of law and order, I don't want to be a witness to anything like this, much as it's deserved."

Amos Clebe rode away, kicking his horse in the ribs, the skirts of his long, black linen coat flapping around his fat legs.

"Let's get this over with," Mike Bastrop said harshly. "The Judge is right. No use hangin' him." He pointed a finger at Kinky Bob. "Slope out of here, you. This is no place for you to linger."

Kinky Bob did not stir his horse. "I'm stayin'," he said. He was inviting death by his defiance and knew it. He had seen men of his race shot down for less.

Bastrop gazed at him with deadly speculation. Whatever the pros and cons that he weighed, the decision went in favor of the black man's survival.

"Stay and be damned," Bastrop said. "Maybe it'll be a lesson to you as well as to him."

Lee began fighting. He was sure they were wrong. Clemmy O'Neil was wrong. She had lied. This, no doubt, was her way of paying him off for humiliating her with the hostler watching. Chances were she had found his watch in the livery.

He wrested free of Bill Tice's grasp. But it was no use. The three Tices piled on him. Their weight carried him to the ground.

Mike Bastrop, from the saddle, flipped a loop around his ankles and yanked it tight. Bastrop gigged his horse and Lee found himself being dragged through brush. His shirt was ripped. Thorns drove into him. Rocks punished him.

He had no real strength to fight back. He was spread-eagled against a dead tree.

Merl Tice got his wish. He was the first to use the quirt. Lee felt the heavy, brutal force of the lash. Felt it strike again. And again.

He saw Kinky Bob, still mounted, gazing at him. It seemed to him that Kinky Bob was also feeling each blow of the lash. It was as though he was trying to add his own power of endurance to Lee's.

Gabe used the quirt also. Their father took a turn. Kinky Bob cried, "In God's mercy! Dat's enough!"

Mike Bastrop spoke. "I reckon that'll do, men." Bastrop was ashen and beads of cold sweat stood on his forehead.

The punishment ceased. Bastrop dismounted, came to where Lee was sagging, seized him by the hair, and twisted his head around. "Get out of this country, Comanche," he said. "Don't let sunrise find you in the Punchbowl. You got off lucky this time. Go back where you came from. To the people that murdered my wife."

They rode away. Kinky Bob cut Lee free and supported him until his knees steadied. Lee made his way to the ditch, waded in, and let the cooling water wash away some of the blood, some of the pain. Kinky Bob doctored the welts on his back, using a cooling ointment they carried in the medical kit.

"What you aim to do, Jack-Lee?" Kink finally asked.

"You know the answer to that, Kink."

Kinky Bob sighed. "I'm afeared I do. I see it in your face. You ain't a forgivin' man."

"One thing kept me from passin' out," Lee said. "It was the thought that I had to live through it, live through anything so as to give them a taste of the same medicine."

"They'll only kill you. Hang you, Jack-Lee. Maybe torture you."

"I want to see how much Merl Tice will take before he caves in. And Gabe. They're tough. But how tough? I'll find out. And their father used a quirt on me, too."

"Vengeance is fer de Lawd, Jack-Lee."

"The Tices aren't the only ones. There are others."

"You mean *him*, don't you, Jack-Lee? De Majah?"

Lee didn't answer that. No answer was needed. Mike Bastrop had not actually swung the quirt, but he had refused to defend Lee or seek a fair hearing.

Then there was Clementina O'Neil. If that was her way of paying him back for the episode at the livery, she had more than succeeded.

He stumbled to where his roan was picketed and picked up his saddle.

"Where you goin'?" Kinky Bob asked.

"It's better that you don't know," Lee said. "You'll hear from me some day."

"Take me along, Jack-Lee. With you gone, there's no friend o' Kinky Bob's here at Verde."

"I'd be doing you no favor, letting you go with me."

"You cain't ride off like dis—nothin' but de clothes on yore back."

"That's about how I came here. At least I own my own horse. And my own packhorse. Where is that buckskin devil? If he's handy, I'll take him with me tonight."

"He handy. I fetched him in from de range along with yore roan. I'll bring him in."

Kink rode away into the early dusk and presently returned, leading a tough, short-coupled buckskin. He accompanied Lee to the ranch bunkhouse and waited moodily while Lee collected his personal belongings and loaded them on the buckskin, which had been equipped with a packsaddle.

The big man went to his shack and made up a pack of food and blankets from his larder. He added a skillet, Dutch oven, and a battered coffeepot. Also an ax, a water bag, and a skinning knife.

"Make sure you got yore razah," he advised. "An' soap an' such. A man feels more like a man if'n he keeps shaved an' lookin' respectable. Then he *stays* respectable."

"That might take more than a razor and soap," Lee said.

"I got more grub cached out in the brush," Kink said. "An' other possibles. Keep dat in mind in case o' need."

"Thanks, my friend," Lee said. They shook hands, and Lee rode off into the darkness.

He had been deadlined out of the range where he had been raised, deadlined by the man he had hoped would come to look on him as a son. Kink had been right. Mike Bastrop hated him. At first there might have been a doubt in Bastrop's mind, but, evidently, as the years passed, he had become certain that Lee was a member of the tribe that had murdered his wife.

Lee began mapping his future. To the west lay the Pecos. Except for stage stations at the few fords, the only habitations along the lonely river were the dugouts of Indian traders or professed hunters who were in reality men hiding from the law, or road agents who preyed on whatever quarry they found on the few trails. Outlaw country. Law officers rarely crossed the Pecos, except in numbers, and usually returned empty-handed and often with empty saddles.

A man with vengeance in his mind could operate from beyond the Pecos. But a man who crossed the river was a lost soul. He had only one course—to become as savage and harsh as the land itself. It was said that, even in the days of the great herds, not even the hardy buffalo had ever grazed west of the Pecos.

Southward was Mexico. A land where a man could take a new name, cloak himself in a new life, and erase the past from his memory. Mexico was a place for forgetting, if a man really wanted to forget.

Eastward lay another lonely land that men avoided. The Llano Estacado it had been named by the early Spanish travelers. The fenced plains. Ranchers called that area the Staked Plains. By either name it was a bitter land—a wasteland where lay the bleached bones of the buffalo that had grazed there, and the bones of soldiers and explorers and Indians who had died there of starvation or thirst, or had frozen in the blizzards that howled across its swells in winter.

To Lee's knowledge no cowboy had ventured more than a few miles beyond the high, dry bluffs that frowned down on the range east of the Armadillo Hills. That particular area of the Staked Plains was written off as a waterless desert for a hundred miles, swept by sandstorms. Punch-bowl people called that area the Devil's Garden.

However, it had been from the Devil's Garden that the Comanches had come in the days of the war trail, sweeping down on the border settlements to scalp and pillage.

No white man had ever crossed the Devil's Garden, it was said. But the Comanches had traveled it, and Lee, as a child, had crossed it with war and hunting parties. He knew its secrets.

If he was to need a hideout, it would be the Devil's Garden. With that decided, he set his course in the direction of BT ranch. After a few miles, he camped for the night in thick brush.

He remained camped until twilight the next day. Saddling the roan, he left the buckskin on picket in the brush and headed toward the Tice ranch. He had treated the welts on his back. They would require attention for a time, but he doubted if there would be any permanent damage.

It was still early evening when he came in sight of the sprawling, many-winged Tice place. Windows in the main section glowed with light, but the bunkhouse, which stood a distance away, was dark. The riders were still in town, spending their pay and trying to forget that the majority of them would soon be heading for Kansas again, riding the harsh miles of the trail.

A late cattle drive was a gamble, but it paid off, if successful. If caught by an early winter, such herds could be held along the Brazos or the Red River, but that meant extra crew expenses and the possibility of loss from blizzards.

Although Bill Tice gambled with Mike Bastrop on these drives and had at least a quarter interest in the bags of gold that had lain on the big table in Casa Bonita the previous day, Lee had been told by old-timers that the man didn't know any more about the art of raising cattle than a hog did about ballroom dancing. And never would, they had always added with a sniff of scorn.

Bill Tice had a gift for gab and impressing the ladies. He had always seemed to find time to spend in town and the money to be well-dressed and barbered, even though what few cattle he had owned in the early days had been scrub stock, afflicted by worms and ticks.

Rose O'Neil's older sister had been an unsophisticated girl of eighteen who was dazzled by Bill Tice's surface manners. She had died within two years after their marriage of neglect and a broken heart. Bill Tice had soon remarried. His second wife had born him two sons before succumbing also to hardship and loneliness at the squalid ranch in the hills.

However, a change had come in Bill Tice's fortunes some years in the past. Some said it was the death of his second wife that had caused him to turn over a new leaf. Whatever the reason, Bill Tice and his ranch began to prosper. Mike Bastrop, who had inherited Rancho Verde after the death of his wife at the hands of Comanches, began to find better qualities in his neighbor than other Punchbowl people had seen. He helped Bill Tice grade up his cattle and widen his range by installing windmills and tanks and check dams along the flanks of the Armadillos.

Within a few years, Rancho Verde and BT were in a pool that was a virtual partnership. An imposing ranch house stood on the site of the former tumble-down house where two wives had died. It was said that Bill Tice had leveled the shack and plowed under the soil so that he would never be reminded of his days of poverty.

He kept adding to the house each year. It was now an amazing polyglot maze of wings and galleries and turrets and gables. He built new wings and rooms on the structure constantly. Cowboys rode far out of their way to take a look at the bizarre collection. It was said there were more than thirty rooms in the place that had never even been occupied.

There was a superstition that some of those rooms were inhabited by the ghosts of the wives Bill Tice had buried. And it was said that Clemmy O'Neil's mother also haunted BT ranch. There were freighters and mule packers who had stopped near BT overnight who declared they had heard Rose O'Neil singing in the midnight blackness. More practical persons said that what those fools had heard was Clemmy O'Neil, who had a voice almost as sweet as that of the Golden Nightingale.

Lee had never been inside the huge ranch house. Ahead, it bulked enormously in the starlight as he dismounted and picketed his horse. It crouched beneath a full moon that was ballooning above the Armadillos, as yellow as a jack-o'-lantern. There were several wings, separated from the original main house by roofed galleries and breezeways.

The original house, where the lights burned, was where the Tices held forth. Lee moved cautiously into the ranch yard on foot and scouted the place.

He could hear voices and the clatter of dishes and utensils. He moved to the east wall and stepped silently into the shadow of the gallery. The curtains of the main room had not been drawn.

Bill Tice, Mike Bastrop, and Judge Amos Clebe sat at a big, linen-spread table which bore the residue of a meal along with wine and whisky bottles and glasses. Mexican servants moved about. Bill Tice, flushed with liquor, embraced a comely servant girl, who escaped, giggling, from his grasp. Amos Clebe, his fat, bearded face expressionless, sat toying with a whisky glass. Mike Bastrop was smoking a cigar and had a wineglass in front of him.

A smaller table in a corner of the room bore poker chips and a deck of cards. There were three chairs at this table. Evidently the game that had started at Rancho Verde had been adjourned to Bill Tice's ranch.

Tice tried to arise drunkenly to pursue the giggling girl who was little more than a child. Mike Bastrop moved. He placed a big hand against Tice's face and shoved him roughly back in his chair. "You're drunk, Bill," he said scornfully. "Swill some coffee instead of booze. Sober up, so we can play a few more hands."

Bill Tice wore the garb of a gentleman—a dark sack coat, white shirt, and string tie. He had a black-velvet sash around his waist in the Spanish style. A pistol and a dagger with a carved gold handle were thrust in the sash.

The two men sat glaring at each other. Bill Tice wanted to go for a weapon but didn't have the courage. Mike Bastrop, who had his six-shooter in a holster on his thigh, smiled mockingly as though daring the BT owner to come at him. Tice quieted and carefully let his hand drop away from his sash.

Judge Clebe had made no move to interfere. When he saw that the crisis was past, he reached for a bottle and refilled his whisky glass. His pale blue eyes did not seem to change expression. However, Lee had the impression that the Judge was disappointed.

Lee moved to a better position which gave him a full view of the table. He discovered that Merl and Gabe Tice were also guests at the supper. The brothers were scowling at Mike Bastrop, but that was as far as they went in resenting his treatment of their father. In fact, Lee believed Merl and Gabe had rather enjoyed seeing their parent humiliated, even though they seemed to hold no particular regard for Mike Bastrop.

Clemmy O'Neil was present at the feast. She sat at the far end of the table, as distant as possible from the others. She wore a modest supper dress and had her hair done in a mature style, but there was taut distaste for her companions in the set of her lips and in the way she stonily ignored them with her eyes. Lee surmised she was here against her will.

She waved away a servant bearing wine. Her glass was turned down. Merl reached across the table, righted the glass, and angrily motioned the servant to fill it.

"Drink up, honey!" he demanded, his voice carrying through the open window. "Here's a toast to the prettiest gal in New Mexico. Come on! Let's clink glasses."

He held the glass to her lips. She suddenly seized it and tossed the contents into his face.

"Why you little hussy!" he exploded. He seized her wrist and started to drag her to her feet.

Mike Bastrop spoke. "Sit down, Merl, before I blow an ear off you."

Bastrop had his six-shooter in his hand. He was one of the best pistol shots in the Punchbowl and usually won the target shooting at the Christmas and Fourth of July festivals.

Merl subsided abruptly. "I was just funnin'," he growled, and went back to his seat. "No need for peelin' out a hog laig on me, Major."

"You carry your funning too far," Bastrop said. "You said she was a sister to you. Treat her as such."

"You know I didn't mean that," Merl growled. "She's not of my blood. You know what she is."

"Shut up!" his father roared, seizing a chance to show authority over his son. "An' I warn you not to try no foolishness with her. You'll git your eyes scratched out. I don't want no scandals in my house."

"Let's go back to the game," Mike Bastrop said. "We've all drunk too much already. What we need is action."

Clemmy O'Neil walked from the room. She walked with dignity, but Lee sensed that she was deathly afraid and wanted to run.

Gabe and Merl downed their drinks and pushed back their chairs. "It's too danged early to turn in," Gabe said. "I'm goin' to town an' maybe play a little monte. How about you, Merl?"

Merl laughed sneeringly. "That monte game wouldn't be at Pedro's place where that little, black-eyed señorita who calls herself Lola Vasquez hangs out, now would it?"

"You ridin' with me or do you just want to keep runnin' off the mouth?"

"I got nobody in Punchbowl I figure worth ridin' fifteen miles to take a look at tonight. I'm turnin' in."

"An' you better do the same, Gabe," his father blustered. "I've heard of Lola Vasquez. An' nothin' good. There ought to be decent girls you can take up with. You hang around that Mexican tamale an' some day you'll likely get a chiv between yore ribs."

Gabe ignored him and stamped out. Lee retreated around a corner of the structure and waited until Gabe had saddled and headed away toward town. By that time Bastrop, the Judge, and Bill Tice were back at their poker game.

Merl Tice came to the front gallery, smoking a cigaret while he watched his brother ride away. Presently Merl headed away through the house, evidently bound for his quarters to turn in for the night.

Lamplight showed in two windows in an east wing of the sprawl of rooms. Lee decided that marked Clemmy O'Neil's rooms. He debated whether to stalk Merl, confront him, and pay him off for the quirt whipping. That was what he had come here to do.

But Clemmy O'Neil was also on his list. There could hardly be physical punishment of a girl, of course, but he at least meant to confront her, and force her to admit she had lied.

He waited until sure Merl was out of the way, then

moved to the wing where the light showed. It was separated from the main building by a roofed, tile-floored patio, which was more popularly known as a dogtrot.

Light seeped around the curtains of the windows. They were casements, open for the sake of coolness. The curtains moved slightly in the draw of the warm breeze. One window overlooked the dogtrot. An arched, wide doorway led into a red-tiled hall that served all the rooms in this wing. The heavy double doors stood open.

Lee crouched beneath the window. He could hear movement inside the room. The rustle of garments. He tiptoed into the hall and to the first door. He put his ear to the panel; the faint footsteps he could hear inside were those of a woman. Clemmy O'Neil, beyond a doubt.

He debated it for a time. From the main wing came the muted sounds of the poker game—the riffle of cards, the clack of chips, an occasional word from the players.

He made his decision. With painful care, he tried the wrought-iron thumb latch that held the heavy cedar portal. The door did not yield. It was bolted inside.

Despite his caution, the latch gave a faint sound as he released pressure. Sounds in the room ceased instantly. He could hear the drive of his own pulse. Or was it the frightened pound of Clemmy O'Neil's lungs he was hearing? He could imagine her terror.

She spoke, so afraid her voice was faint and shaky. "Merl? Is that you?"

Lee did not answer. He began slowly, soundlessly drawing away from the door, taking a backward step at a time.

She spoke again. "Merl? If it *is* you, go away!" She added quaveringly, "I've got a gun. I'll use it! You know I will!"

On a sudden hunch, Lee spoke softly. "It isn't Merl."

There was a space of silence. Then she said, "It's Lee Jackson, isn't it." It was more a statement than a question.

To Lee's surprise, the bolt in the door grated and the door opened. He stared. In the short time since she had left the main room she had changed from the supper costume to denim riding breeches and boots, a cotton shirtwaist, and a neckerchief. A false riding skirt lay on a chair, ready to be pinned around her waist as a sop to convention which considered riding astride unladylike.

She had rearranged her hair in a tight, coiled plait, so that it would fit beneath her sombrero which lay on the bed. She had a pistol in her hand, her finger on the trigger. It was a short-muzzled .32, such as might be carried in a purse or handbag. At this range it could be very deadly.

She did not point the gun at him. She merely gazed at him, waiting, her eyes jade green with the stress of her emotions.

She studied him for a time. Then, as though satisfied of something, she motioned him to enter. "Quick!" she murmured. "Someone might see you!"

Astounded, Lee stepped into the room. She closed the door. He saw that this was a sitting room, comfortably furnished with easy chairs, sofa, books, an oil reading lamp, and rag rugs.

An open door led to a bedroom, where the sombrero lay. A bedroll was lashed in a tarp for packing on a saddle.

"You act like you might have been expecting me," Lee said.

"Maybe I was," she responded. She kept her voice down to a whisper.

Lee followed that example. "Don't you know it's bad luck to put a hat on a bed."

"I'm not superstitious," she said.

"Why did you figure I'd come here?" he asked.

"I heard what happened yesterday. They whipped you."

"That ought to have made you happy."

"Happy? What sort of a person do you think I am?"

"I wonder. What sort of a person would do what you did to get square? I'm sorry about kissing you. I apologize. I was drunk. I didn't really mean to."

"You mean no man would kiss Clemmy O'Neil unless he was full of booze and didn't know what he was doing?"

Lee cocked an eyebrow. "You said that. I didn't. At any rate, I don't figure it was worth fixing to have me flogged and run out of the country. They might even have strung me up. That's what usually happens to a man accused of what you said I did."

He added, "You lied, didn't you?"

"This is why I knew you'd come here," she said. "To tell me I lied. That's why I guessed you were the one outside my door just now."

She was continually jabbing him off balance by her coolness. "Better put that gun down," he said. "You might touch it off and hurt somebody."

She lowered the gun slightly. "That's better," he said. "They've deadlined me out of the Punchbowl, because of what you told them. But I'm not leaving. I'll hang around. You can tell Merl and Gabe that. And their father. They were the ones who swung the whip on me. Tell them that sooner or later they'll know how it feels."

"I don't suppose you'd believe me if I told you I had nothing to do with it," she said. "I never said you were the man who broke into my room that night."

"The Tices told it different."

"They were the ones who lied," she said. "Someone did come in here that night. Through the window. I had gone to bed. I heard him. He had a pillowcase over his head, with eyeholes cut in it. He grabbed me and we fought. I managed to scream like a banshee. That scared him away. He scrambled back through the window and got away before anybody showed up to help me."

She added, after a space of silence, "I never said you were the man. It was Merl who found your watch in my room."

She paused again, then remarked, "At least he *said* he had found it there."

Lee eyed her questioningly. She nodded. "I'm sure it was Merl in that pillowcase. I've been afraid of him for a long time. He came back from town in a wild rage that night after I'd been in Punchbowl. The hostler had told him about seeing you kiss me. He was like a wild man. He accused me of awful things. He said he'd make you the sorriest man alive."

"He almost did," Lee said.

"You don't want to believe me, do you?" she asked.

The trouble was that Lee *did* find himself believing her, against his will. Evidently the hostler had found his watch and had given it to Merl Tice when he had gone to Merl with the story of what had happened in the livery.

She was watching him. "I could be lying, of course,"

she said. "I could be stringing you along so that you won't harm me to pay off for what they did to you at the horse camp. That's why you came here, wasn't it?"

"Maybe," Lee said.

"That's why I expected you," she said.

"I wanted to get a close look at a girl who'd tell a lie like that," Lee admitted.

"Are you getting a close enough look?"

"Closer than an Indian is supposed to look at even—"

He broke off. He hadn't meant to say anything like that.

She said to him. "—at even a person like Clemmy O'Neil. About the only thing lower than Clemmy O'Neil is an Indian."

"Again you're the one who said that, not me," Lee said.

"Some things need saying."

CHAPTER FOUR

Lee eyed her garb and gazed around at the evidence of preparations for a journey. "You going somewhere?" he asked.

"I'm leaving BT," she said.

"For keeps?"

"For keeps."

"You don't like it here?"

She gave him a wry smile. "That's putting it mildly."

"Where will you go?"

"That's none of your concern," she said.

The sounds from the poker game had become more audible. The voices of the players had risen. They were in angry dispute.

"It's Bastrop and Bill Tice again," Lee said. "They don't seem to be the pals everybody thinks they are. I saw the Major push Bill Tice in the face at the supper table. I was peeking at a window."

"Window peepers can get shot," she said.

"I'd say, from the sounds, that somebody else might get shot," Lee remarked. "What caused 'em to fall out?"

"They're always quarreling," she said. "But that's as far as it goes. They despise each other."

"But they're partners."

She shrugged. "Wolves run in packs. And eat each other if the chance comes."

"I hear they play for big stakes," Lee said. "And they say the Major loses pretty heavy to the Judge and Bill Tice."

"Bosh!" she sniffed.

"What do you mean, 'bosh'?"

"All three of them are so miserly they wouldn't risk more than a few dollars in a card game."

"What? But everybody says—"

"I know. Everybody thinks thousands of dollars change hands in those games. If so, I've never seen it. They like to play poker, but only to pass time. But none of them wants to lose. They're that kind."

"How do you know this?" Lee demanded.

"I spy on them. I'm a window peeper, too. I've spied on them since I was a child. Uncle Tice caught me at it years ago, and beat me. Oh, how he beat me. I couldn't sit down for days. He told me it would go harder on me if he ever caught me eavesdropping on him and his friends again."

She gave him another of her little, dry smiles. "Since then I've been more careful. He hasn't caught me at it."

Clemmy O'Neil was no longer speaking in the brittle, superior manner that Lee associated with her. He understood suddenly that this had been a defensive armor, the image she showed to a world that was trying always to snub her.

Her voice was clear, musical. There was a Spanish flavor to the way she formed her words. This was due, no doubt, to her training at the convent and at the hands of Mexican housekeepers at the Tice ranch.

The sounds of quarreling faded. But the poker game was not being resumed.

The girl moved to the window and listened. "They're finally quitting," she said. "Major Bastrop and the Judge are leaving." She added, "You must wait. They'll be gone in a few minutes."

Lee scowled at her. She was as much as dismissing him, and even directing when he should leave. She seemed to be taking it for granted that he believed the story she had told about the intruder in the pillowcase.

He waited. Bill Tice was bawling an order for the Judge's buggy and Mike Bastrop's horse to be brought up. A wrangler evidently was still on call.

"What will you do?" Clemmy O'Neil asked as they waited.

Lee shrugged. "*Quien sabe?* I haven't decided."

She was silent for a time. "I think you *do* know," she said abruptly. "You've made up your mind." She added, "Don't do it!"

"Do what?"

"Become an outlaw. How is it they say it, ride the trail where the owls hoot?"

"What makes you think I'd do a thing like that?" Lee demanded.

"It's written on you. You've already taken the first step."

"And what was this first step?"

"You didn't come to this ranch to window peep. You came here to pay off for what they did to you. To use force. What will be your next step? And the next?"

"You aim to preach to me?" Lee snapped.

"Now that would be something, wouldn't it?" she replied. "Clemmy O'Neil preaching, standing up for the straight and narrow path. Isn't that a big laugh?"

Beneath her mockery was pathos and loneliness. That angered Lee. "For God's sake!" he exploded. "Don't start pitying yourself! Not you, of all people. Don't let them break you!"

She straightened, stung. The defiance returned. "I don't pity myself," she said. "And nobody will ever break me. I'll promise you that."

"Nor me," Lee said. "And that's another promise."

He heard the crunch of wheels and hoofs as Amos Clebe's buggy and Mike Bastrop's mount were brought to the front of the house.

Bill Tice's voice sounded. "Be careful, Clebe, you old sot. You'll bust a laig gettin' into that buggy if you ain't careful. Maybe I better tie you down in that thing, else you might fall out and break your fat neck. You can sleep it off while the horse takes you home."

Lee heard stealthy movement in the hall. Clemmy O'Neil heard it also. Someone was at the door. The latch was being tested. The door was opening slightly. She had failed to bolt it after Lee had entered the room.

Lee drew his .44. She gave him a frightened look, then moved to the lamp on the dressing table and blew out the light. "Who's there?" she called.

The door swung open. Faint light seeped in from the windows in the main house. The intruder had a pillowcase over his head. From his size, Lee was certain it was Merl Tice.

He holstered his six-shooter. Reaching out in the darkness, he caught the intruder by his mask, dragged him into the room, and kicked the door closed.

He sent a fist smashing into the face beneath the mask.

He struck again, and a third time. He was remembering the agony of the quirt Merl had wielded on his back. He felt a measure of fierce, primitive satisfaction as his fists crashed into bone and flesh. At least part of the debt was being paid.

His target was smashed to the floor and out of his grasp. The masked man was Merl Tice, right enough. Merl mumbled in a shocked voice, "My God! Is that you, Gabe? It's me. Merl. Don't hit me ag'in. I'm—"

Merl must have realized that he might not be talking to his brother. He probably was armed and reaching for his gun. Lee could not chance an attempt to locate him in the darkness. If they began trying to find each other with bullets, Clemmy O'Neil might be in the line of fire.

Lee jerked the door open, ran into the hallway and out of the building.

Merl Tice raised a frantic shout. "Stop him! Paw! Major Bastrop! There's a man runnin'! Stop him! Shoot him!"

Lee veered, followed the shadow of a gallery, and circled two sections of the sprawling maze of wings and additions. He paused in shadows against a wall.

Merl's voice was rising to almost a scream. "You trollop! Who was it you had in here? I'll kill him! I'll roast him over a slow fire! He's broke my nose. Knocked out my teeth. I'll skin him alive!"

Merl added, his voice rising still higher in a burst of fury, "It was that damned Comanch', wasn't it? Lee Jackson! I might have knowed!"

Merl's screeching was bringing answering shouts from his father and Mike Bastrop. Lee could hear them running, but they were confused as to direction.

Lee retreated to the west side of the house. He could hear them concentrating on the east wing. A man ran past, within a dozen feet of where he crouched, but kept going to join in the confusion on the opposite side of the buildings. Lee guessed it was the wrangler who had returned to the bunkhouse after rigging the Judge's harness horse and Mike Bastrop's mount.

Lee darted across the open ranch yard and reached a haystack. From there he made his way to the barn. He crouched there, trying to suppress his breathing. He could still hear Merl making wild explanations.

Then he heard them scatter. The search was on. A man came running from a dogtrot into the open ranch yard. It was Bill Tice. He had a pistol in his hand. He halted, peering around, crouching slightly as he tried to pick up any sign of movement in the shadows or any sound.

A gun flamed from the dogtrot not thirty feet beyond where Bill Tice stood. It roared again. And a third time. The shots were spaced a second or two apart, as though the marksman was making very sure of his target.

Lee had the impression the flashes came from the window of Clemmy O'Neil's sitting room which opened onto the dogtrot. The reports were lighter than would have come from the .44s that most men carried, or even a .38. Lee was remembering the .32-caliber pistol that Clemmy O'Neil owned.

He heard each slug smash into Bill Tice's body. The sounds were like the spaced blows of a hammer on wood.

Bill Tice uttered a choking moan. He gasped, "Don't— don't—! Oh, my God! I've always been afeared you'd—"

Bill Tice was reeling as he spoke. He fell on his face and Lee could hear the agonized wheezing fade away as his life ended there in the dust.

Lee circled the barn and retreated from the ranch, keeping the barn between himself and the scene of the murder.

For it had been murder! The person who had fired the shots could not have been mistaken as to the identity of his target.

Wild shouting arose again in the BT ranch yard. Lee could hear Amos Clebe's voice, shocked and shrill. And Mike Bastrop's deeper tones.

Merl was shouting, "It's Paw! He's dead! He's dead!"

Again Merl's voice rose to a frenzied screech. "That hellcat! That vixen! She's the cause of this! Maybe she even done it herself! She hated Paw! I'll tear her to pieces!"

Lee had started to circle to where he had left his horse. He paused and stood listening. The sounds indicated that Merl was raging through the rambling ranch house in search of Clemmy O'Neil. He heard Judge Clebe trying to calm the infuriated man.

Merl would not listen. "Where are you, Clemmy?" he

yelled. "You can't hide so deep I can't find you an' drag you out! Where are you?"

Lee heard the sudden pound of hoofs of a spurred horse. Mike Bastrop's voice sounded, "She's taken my horse and is pulling out!"

The rider came in Lee's direction. A mounted figure loomed against the stars. Clemmy O'Neil was astride with the false skirt adding to her mount's wildness.

The horse reared when it saw Lee in its path and nearly unseated the girl. She had a pistol in her hand and was trying to bring it to bear on him.

"Don't shoot!" Lee exclaimed. "It's Lee Jackson!"

"Get out of the way!" she panted. "They'll be after me. They'll kill me!"

She added, "And they'll hang you for sure, now. Why did you do it?"

"Do what?"

"Why did you shoot Uncle Tice?"

"Me?" The horse reared again and tried to strike Lee with its hoofs. He caught a grip on the saddle and vaulted up behind the girl.

"Let's ride!" he said. "We'd make a pretty pair, strung up together for buzzard bait, now wouldn't we?"

She had no alternative, for he clamped his left arm around her waist and slapped the horse into motion. It was a big, powerful black with thoroughbred blood in it, the pick of Mike Bastrop's stock. He slapped the animal into a gallop.

"I heard Merl say that maybe it was you who killed his Paw," he said.

She began trying to talk, but she was weeping and unintelligible. Evidently no one at the ranch had been able to mount pursuit as yet. Lee took the reins from Clemmy O'Neil's shaking hands and guided the way to where he had left his roan. His horse was still grazing peacefully on picket. He slid from the black and swung into the saddle.

"Where are you going?" she asked.

"I'm going to where the owls hoot," Lee said. "That's where you said I would wind up. As for you, we'll cross the trail to town a mile or so ahead. You can ride into Punchbowl. You'll be safe there. At least from Merl Tice."

"Safe! Safe! I'll never be safe as long as any Tice is alive. Only from Uncle Tice. And that's because he's dead! And then there's that slimy Judge Clebe and—and that awful Major Bastrop!" She was hysterical, frenzied.

"What do you mean?" Lee demanded. "Amos Clebe and Mike Bastrop? Why would you be afraid of them?"

"They suspect I know too much because I eavesdropped on them," she wept.

"Too much about what?"

"About why they play poker and never really win or lose, I suppose."

"You suppose? Don't you know? Why don't they ever win or lose?"

"I don't know!" she blubbered. "And quit pestering me. I tell you I don't know. And I'm too tired to talk about it."

"Then where can you go?" Lee demanded.

She dabbed at her eyes in the darkness. "You tell me."

Lee peered closer at her. "Oh, no you don't!" he exclaimed. "You're going to Punchbowl!"

"You wouldn't really want me to do that."

"*Me?* Why not?"

"You ought to be able to figure that out, Lee Jackson. I'm the only person who really knows that you were the man who slugged Merl in my room. They'll try to force me to tell who it was."

"Oh, so it's me you're worrying about," Lee snorted. "Merl guessed right from the start that I was the one who gave him that beating."

"It takes more than a guess to convict a man of murder."

"Murder?" Lee seized her arm, shaking her. "Are you still trying to pretend that I killed Bill Tice?"

She refused to answer. His grip tightened, but she would not ask for mercy, although he heard her draw a sharp breath.

"I ought to drag you off that horse and set you afoot," he raged. "Bill Tice was shot by someone at the house. I saw the flashes. They came from inside the dogtrot. Just where *were* you at the time?"

"I tell you I didn't do it."

"I'm asking where you were. Or don't you have an answer thought up?"

"I—I don't know where I was," she wailed.

"Now you don't expect me to believe that."

"I don't expect you to believe anything good about me. I followed Merl when he ran out to chase you after you had left. Merl had a gun and would have killed you. Then the shooting broke out. I thought it came from the other side of the house, for I was some distance away. Merl ran in that direction by way of the front of the place. I decided I'd better go back to my room. Then Merl began screaming that Uncle Tice had been killed and that I was to blame. He was coming to get me. So I ran back to the front of the house, took Major Bastrop's horse, and rode away."

When Lee remained silent, she took that for disbelief. She pulled away from his grasp. "I don't care whether you believe me or not," she cried. "It's the truth. Don't you dare try to twist things around to make it out that I'm lying."

"There's always been talk that Bill Tice found a gold mine when he became your guardian," Lee said. "Some people believe your mother wasn't as penniless as advertised."

"I'm sure Uncle Tice has robbed me blind," she said grimly. "It's only been since I grew up that I realized it. Now, it's probably too late."

"You told me you were afraid of all the Tices. Of your uncle, especially. He was shot with a small-bore gun. I'm sure of that. You had a purse-gun in your hand when I saw you in your room. Isn't that the same gun you've got in your belt now? Let's take a look at it."

She suddenly struck him in the face. She had little strength and the blow did no damage. It was like a frightened child lashing out at fear itself—at a phantom in a nightmare.

"You're trying to build up quite a case against me, aren't you?" she choked. "Don't try to touch me. I'll shoot you. It's clear enough. You killed him and intend to put it on me."

Lee drew away from her. "I'm not trying to put anything on you that doesn't belong on your conscience," he said. "Bill Tice was shot in the back. Deliberately. Coolly. *That* is why it was murder."

The wagon trail that led to town loomed ahead in the moonlight. "You better go into town," Lee said. "Go to the sheriff. Tell him your story. Tell the truth. They say Fred Mack is an honest man."

"But he's a man, isn't he? And I'm the daughter of Rose O'Neil. Every man seems to want to paw over me. He'd send me back to BT, most likely. Gabe and Merl are there. That'd be even worse."

"But—"

"Let's face it," she said. "I can put your neck in a noose, Lee Jackson. You know you wouldn't have a chance if I testified that you came into my room tonight to get even for the whipping they gave you. Merl would testify against you. Who'd believe your word against even the likes of me? Everybody says you're a—a—"

"Comanche," Lee said. "And I've decided they're right."

"Right or wrong, we've got to hide someplace. They'll trail us. Where can we go?"

"I tell you that you can't go with me."

"We're two of a kind. Dirt under their feet. You had already made up your mind to ride long. There's no other choice for me. If you're an outlaw, so am I."

Lee began another refusal, but she halted him. "I'm staying with you whether you want it that way or not. It's all I can do. I don't like it any better than you do. You must know of a hiding place. Otherwise you wouldn't have come to the BT tonight. You meant to pay off the Tices for what they did. You knew you'd be trailed and maybe hanged if they caught you. You're wasting time trying to send me back. I would only follow you."

She was right, of course. Every minute lost in debate meant that pursuit would be closer on his heels by daybreak. Circumstances forced him to let her have her way. For the present at least.

He urged the roan ahead. "All right," he said. "You've asked for it. Here we go."

He set a steady pace until they reached the thicket where he had left the buckskin and his camp gear. Leading the packhorse, they pushed on.

They had not spoken in nearly an hour. "If you don't mind, you might get rid of that cussed thing that keeps flapping like the wings of an owl," Lee finally said. "Your horse doesn't like it one bit, and neither does mine."

She removed the false skirt and bundled it on the

saddle. "But I'll wear it in daylight," she said. "The horses will have to get used to it. I don't feel decent, riding like a man."

"This is hardly the time to get choosy," Lee commented.

"I imagine I can find a store somewhere, so I can buy myself a dress or two," she said. "I had to leave without taking any of the clothes I'd laid out. I'll need a few other things, too."

"Store? Do you know what you're saying?"

"Oh, I see," she said. "I forgot. We just can't ride into some town and go shopping."

"Not unless you want to go to jail. But there are other ways of getting what we need."

"How do you mean to—?" she began. Then she understood. Again she said, "I see." She said it slowly, wearily.

"You gave it a name a while back," Lee said. "Outlaw. That's what we are. Outlaws. But you don't seem to have given much thought to what it really meant."

"I'm afraid not," she said. "But I'm learning."

They said nothing more for a long time. They reached Flat Creek near the Armadillo Hills after midnight and followed its bed of heavy gravel and bedrock in order to blind their trail. The stream bottom offered tricky going in the patches of moonlight. Hoofs sent water flying, dampening riders as well as animals. However, the night was so warm they both felt refreshed.

After more than an hour of this, Lee let the horses rest and drink. He dismounted and helped Clemmy down.

"We'll take a breather," he said. "How are you making out?"

"If you're asking if I'm tired, the answer is yes. If you're asking if I want to turn back, the answer is no."

They found a sand bar where they could lie on their stomachs, drink, and dip their faces in water. The horses blew noisily downstream.

"How far away are they?" she asked.

"How far away are what?"

"The Staked Plains. I've never been east of the Armadillo Hills, and so I have no idea of distance."

"Who said anything about going into the plains?"

"You didn't have to say it, but I know that's what you've got in your mind."

"And how would you know that?"

"Now, how could I answer that? I'm just guessing, of course. But that's what you're planning, isn't it?"

Lee believed he had the answer. The Staked Plains had always been looked upon as Comanche country. It was into the plains the Spearmen had usually vanished after their raids. A Comanche, in need of a hiding place, would instinctively turn to that refuge even now. She had been aware of all this.

"You don't really believe I'd let you go there, do you?" he asked roughly.

"Not if you could help it, I suppose. They say it's a fearful place. I've heard of the Devil's Garden all my life. But you can't help it. If you feel that you'll be safer there, then I'll feel the same way."

She added, "Hadn't we better be traveling?"

Lee found that he had no grounds on which to debate the matter. He helped her into the saddle of the black horse.

They rode steadily eastward through the night. At daybreak they emerged from the hills into a view of a wild stretch of country. In the distance stood a low, forbidding line of bluffs.

"Caprock," Lee said. "There are your Staked Plains."

"You've been there?" she asked.

"Yes."

"With the Comanches?"

"Yes. As a child, to help flense robes and cure buffalo meat." He added, "And, on one trip, to wait while the warriors went ahead on a raid. They came back with a lot of stolen horses. And scalps."

"But, is there water?" she asked after a pause. "I've been told there's none for miles and miles in the Devil's Garden."

Lee eyed her. "Do you intend to follow me in there?"

"Yes. You don't intend to stay in that awful place all your life, do you?"

"That might depend on how long a man stays alive."

"You can't scare me," she said, but there was a quaver in her voice.

"It'll be weeks before they quit looking for us," Lee said. "Months maybe. They'll see to it that men will be watching for us if we show up beyond the plains in any direction. We might have to tough it out in there for a long time—if you're still bent on making an Indian of yourself."

"Indian?"

"That word does something to you, inside, doesn't it?"

She gave him an icy look. "No. If I were an Indian, I'd be proud of it."

"That's the only way anyone can live in the Garden. The Indian way. You don't stay alive there just by wishing. You work for it. Maybe fight for it."

"Anything would be better than what I'd be up against back there."

Lee reached out, took the .32 pistol from her belt before she realized his intention. He released the cylinder and punched out the shells. There were two live shells and four empties. Three of the exploded cartridges bore fresh powder burns. The fourth was blackened by time and evidently had been carried as a safety under the hammer.

She stared at the evidence. What color there had been in her face faded away as she understood what this meant.

"Do you still want me to believe you didn't shoot Bill Tice?" he asked. "He was hit by three shots from a light-caliber gun."

"It's—it's impossible!" she gasped. "I don't know how ... !" Then a thought occurred to her. Scorn and accusation came into her face.

"Very clever," she said. "I didn't know you were a sleight-of-hand artist."

Lee laughed grimly. "Meaning that I palmed those empty shells in place of live ones? That's too ridiculous to talk about."

He held the gun to the light. "How about the powder stains? This gun was fired recently. I couldn't have done that by hokus-pokus, now could I?"

"I suppose not," she snapped.

Lee waited for further denials, but she turned her back on him and sat rigid and scornful on the horse. It was plain that she had made up her mind to offer no further explanations nor to submit to any more questioning.

He expected her to weaken and decide to turn back, but she kept pace with him, riding in dogged silence all during the stolid heat of the afternoon. He kept to cover

as much as possible, often swinging far out of the dir
line eastward in order to stay below the skyline or
follow stands of brush. Whenever they were forced
cross exposed areas, they dismounted and walked close
the sides of their horses.

"There are lots of mustangs in this country," he sa
"If anybody spots us at a distance, let's hope they figu
they're only seeing a wild horse or two."

The grim bluffs drew closer. Lee knew that she w
peering at them with increasing apprehension.

"How long . . . ?" she finally began, then left it unf
ished.

It was the first word she had spoken since the incide
of the empty cartridges in the pistol.

"How long since I've been on the Llano?" Lee said. "
that what you were going to ask? Two years. I took
paseo there, just to see if it really was like I remember
it."

"And was it?"

"Yes. For all I could tell, nobody had been in the
since the last Comanche war party came down the plai
years ago."

"How was it when you were with—" she hesitated, th
plunged ahead, "—with the Comanches?"

Lee studied it. "With most Comanches it was a go
life. With me it was a different story."

"In what way?"

"Eagle-in-the-Sky, who said he was my father, had
taboo on me. He seemed to be afraid of me. He hated r
for some reason and did his best to make life misera
for me."

"You mean he tortured you? But you were only a chi
I've heard that Indians are very kind to their children."

"Then I was the exception. The one who said she w
my mother was the worst of all. She was Eagle's eld
wife. Her name was Wau-Qua. I never knew what th
stood for in the Comanche language. To me it mea
cruelty."

"What was your name in the Comanche tongue?"

"I don't know. It was never spoken in my presence.
was taboo. Many things are taboo to Indians."

He gazed northward into the distance. "They're still
there. Beyond the Llano. On the Comanche reserve on t

Clear Fork of the Brazos River. I was told a few months ago that Eagle-in-the-Sky is still alive and chief of his village. I had hoped that he was dead."

He looked at her. "There are times when I get to remembering, and then I want to kill him. But he might be telling the truth when he said he was my father."

Clemmy was silenced, frightened by his bitterness.

CHAPTER FIVE

They camped at dark. Clemmy accepted the tarp and blanket Lee handed her and slept in the shelter of a boulder, protected from the wind that changed from warmth to thin chill before dawn. It was a lonely wind, which whispered and moaned in the brush. It drove white clouds across the face of the moon. Clouds that formed phantom shapes.

Lee was soddenly tired, but sleep evaded him for a long time. He lay looking up at the drifting clouds. His life had been like that. Driven this way and that at the whim of savages and white men.

That part of his life was finished. His days of drifting were over. Comanche, Spanish, Mexican, white—whatever his blood, he would not only meet every man eye-to-eye, but would take from them what he needed and what he wanted. By violence, if necessary.

He became aware of faint sounds in the darkness. Clemmy O'Neil was awake also. She lay weeping, trying to silence her grief. She wept for all the slights and wounds that life had inflicted on her.

Lee lifted his head. "There'll be no more tears," he said harshly. "If tears are to be shed, let others do it."

They resumed their journey at dawn. At mid-morning they emerged from a canyon after a hard climb that tired the horses. Before them lay a vast, silent land. Its swells were a frozen sea, extending to the horizon and broken by low buttes and wrinkled hills that were like the hulls of sinking ships.

Neither of them spoke for a time. Clemmy broke the silence. "Lead the way," she said.

There was a new soberness in her. A steadfast quality. Her eyes were gray now, and cool.

Together they rode into the Devil's Garden. The swells

enclosed them. The buttes and eroded hills never came nearer.

At intervals, when Lee believed she was not aware of it, he glanced back.

It was late afternoon when she finally spoke. "Are they still trailing us?"

"I didn't think you knew," Lee said.

"I've known it since morning. I glimpsed them far back on the flats when we were climbing the canyon. And they're gaining."

"They're punishing their horses," Lee said. "They're less than an hour's ride back of us now. If they don't quit soon, I'll discourage 'em."

"It's Gabe and Merl, isn't it?"

"That's my guess," Lee said. "But there are three of them. I think the other one is Mike Bastrop. They seem to be the ones who want us bad enough to follow us into the Garden."

They continued their steady pace for another hour. Their own horses were growing foot-heavy.

"All right," Lee said, pulling up in the shelter of uptilted slabs of rock that shaded them from the westering sun. "You'll be all right here. You know how to use a rifle, I imagine."

"Yes," she said. Her voice was faint, shaky.

"If they show up, keep them at a distance until dark. Shoot their horses. You can get away from them if you put them afoot. Go back to Verde and get in touch with Kink. Do what he tells you. That's about all the advice I can give you."

He took a swallow from the water bag. "There's enough left to get you back to Flat Creek," he said. "Rest the horses a few hours until moon-up. It will be up late, but you can travel farther and faster in the cool."

"I'm going with you," she said.

"No. I intend to come back. But there's always the chance of bad luck. Do you remember that barranca we crossed back there a quarter of a mile or so? It was what I've been looking for all afternoon."

"How?"

"I don't intend to kill them. Only set them afoot like I just told you to do. I'd really be doing them a favor.

They'd never make it out of the Garden if they followed us much farther. They're probably already worse off for water than we are."

He walked away, carrying his rifle. She was still standing in the shade of the rocks, watching, when he looked back before brush intervened.

He descended a broken slant, keeping to cover, and reached a wide, dry flat, sparsely sprinkled with saltbush and rabbit brush. A shallow barranca, cut by runoffs from thunderstorms, curved into the flat from the base of the descent.

He had marked this gully as a likely place for his purpose, for its presence had not been apparent until they were almost upon it.

He made his way along the shallow gully until he came to the point where he and Clemmy had crossed with their mounts and the packhorse. He found a clump of brush growing on the rim which offered an observation point and settled down to wait.

There could be no question but that the pursuers knew they had been sighted by their quarry. Therefore they would be alert, no doubt, for the possibility of an ambush. However, their approach to Lee's hiding place would bring them across nearly half a mile of this unbroken flat which offered little chance of concealment.

He was gambling on the hope they would not discover the presence of the gully until too late. If they did become aware of the danger in time, the tables would be turned. It would be Lee who would be caught in a trap, for, with three of them to deal with, it would only be a matter of time until he would be outflanked and wiped out by crossfire.

Minutes dragged by. Lee chanced another glimpse and hastily withdrew his head. The three riders had appeared. They were still a long rifleshot away. When he chanced another look, they were nearer and miraged by heat refraction and the background of the steel-blue sky to fantastic proportions. Their horses seemed to be walking on stilts, but the riders were flattened to froglike shapes.

Suddenly they took on normal shapes. Merl Tice rode in the lead. Even at that distance Lee could see the white strips of medical plaster that bound his nose and jaw, the result of the beating Lee had given him. He rode with the hungry attitude of a hound on the scent of its quarry. His horse was caked with alkali. The animal was nearing the end of its strength, but was still being pushed by spur and quirt.

Gabe Tice and Mike Bastrop were lagging a trifle, but were being forced to prod their mounts to keep pace with the eager one. Lee sank back out of sight. The route Merl was following would bring the trio to the wash within yards of where he crouched.

Presently he could hear the scuff of hoofs and the creak of saddle leather. Mike Bastrop's voice, surly with weariness, sounded. "Take it easy, I tell you, Merl. What are you trying to do, kill these horses?"

"It's nearin' sundown an' unless we get that Indian before night, he might slip away," Merl answered. "I ain't stoppin' until I get my hands on him an' beat him to a pulp. Turn back if your guts have gone yellow on you, Bastrop. Gabe an' me can handle him. An' that girl, too. It'll be a pleasure."

"Then why didn't you take care of him when he busted that buzzard beak of yours the other night?" Mike Bastrop said scornfully. "If you could fight as big as you talk, I'd let you go on alone. If you ask me, that Comanche devil would make you crawl and whimper if—"

Bastrop's voice broke off. "Look!" he exclaimed. "There's a gully . . . !"

They had discovered the possible danger of an ambush. Lee emerged from concealment. They were less than a hundred feet away and were yanking their jaded horses to a stop.

Bastrop, reacting faster than the Tice brothers, was trying to get at his six-shooter. But he had pushed the holster back and out of position for the sake of comfort.

Lee shouted, "No!"

Bastrop continued to twist, trying to draw his pistol. Lee fired the rifle. The bullet drove through the peak of Bastrop's tall hat. The hat was torn from his head and toppled across the face of his horse.

Bastrop was riding one of his fine black saddle-mounts, a cross of quarterhorse and thoroughbred. The animal was weary, but the gunshot and the flight of the hat brought an explosion. It humped its back instantly and swapped ends, trying to unload its rider.

Bastrop was caught off balance. He grabbed the hor
but was partly unseated. His weight spilled the horse. M
and animal went down in a sprawling fall. The six-shoo
was jolted from Bastrop's holster and fell out of reach.]
lay stunned, a leg caught beneath the horse which h
rolled partly on its back, the saddle wedging it in t
position so that it was unable to right itself immediately.

Lee levered another shell under the hammer. Merl a
Gabe Tice had sat frozen by surprise for a second or tw
They were now making frenzied, belated attempts to
at their weapons. Gabe's choice was a rifle in the boot
his saddle, while Merl's preference was a six-shooter i
holster.

Lee sent a bullet within inches of Gabe's ear. "No!"
shouted again. "Lift your hands!"

The brothers froze. For a space the only sound was
gasping of Mike Bastrop. Then the hands of the two Ti
went suddenly in the air.

"Pile down!" Lee commanded. "On this side! Slc
Keep your hands up!"

The brothers complied, sliding from the saddles w
arms stretched high. They were almost ludicrous in th
stiffness and apprehension.

Mike Bastrop's horse managed to roll into position a
lurch to its feet. It trotted away a few rods, its trail
reins finally bringing it to a halt.

Bastrop, still gagging for breath, located his pistol ly
nearby and scrambled toward it.

His path was blocked by Lee's boots. Lee jammed
boot heel into the man's face, shoved him back, t
picked up the weapon and thrust it in his own belt.

He continued to keep the Tices covered. "T
around," he ordered the brothers. "Keep your ha
high."

When they complied, he moved in and disarmed the
Both had rifles on the saddles. In addition to a six-shoo
Merl's sleeve yielded a slingshot. Gabe had a knife in
armpit holster and a set of brass knuckles in his
pocket.

Lee dropped all the captured weapons into the barr
ca, out of reach. The horses the Tices had been rid
drifted away to join Bastrop's animal.

"Put down that rifle, Jackson," Bastrop said hoars

"We're taking you back to Punchbowl. Alive, if you give up peaceful. Dead, if you want it that way."

"You've got things twisted, Major," Lee said. "It's my choice, not yours. I've decided to let you stay alive—this time at least. You can make it back to Flat Creek by noon tomorrow if you keep walking all night. That's your first chance at water. There's none in the direction I'm heading. So there'd be no point in following me any farther, although I'd be happy to see you try."

They eyed him, their mouths tightening as they realized what this meant. A water bag hung on one of their saddles. Lee walked to the horse, lifted the bag, and tossed it at their feet. It seemed to be more than half filled.

"That's better than you deserve," he said.

He jabbed Merl in the back with the rifle, sending him staggering. "You too, Major," he said. "Walk! On the double!"

He shoved the man into motion. "Not you, Gabe," he said. "You're staying here for a while."

Gabe Tice had started to follow his companions. He paused, scowling, not understanding.

"We've got a matter to settle," Lee said. "You're the last of the three men who used a quirt on me. Merl paid off some of what he owed me the other night when I took a few swings at him while he was wearing that pillowcase over his head. He got off easy that time, but there may come another day. The other of the three is dead. Maybe he's lucky. But you're the one I'm after right now."

Gabe looked at Lee's weapons and his lips were suddenly ashen. "You ain't goin' to kill me like you killed Paw?" he protested, his voice hoarse. "You wouldn't shoot me down without givin' me a chance?"

"If I was going to shoot you, you'd have your chance," Lee said. "And you'll have your chance now. But not with guns. You've got a reputation as a tough man in a fist fight. This is going to be with fists."

Gabe didn't believe him for a moment. Then hope began to rise in him. And distrust. He turned and looked at his brother and at Mike Bastrop who had paused a short distance away and were listening. They, too, apparently were doubting their own ears.

Lee motioned with his rifle. "You two keep going," he said. "You can wait out there a ways if you want. But far enough away so that you won't interfere in this little affair. This is between Gabe and me. Don't stop until you're a long shot away."

It dawned on them that he might actually mean it. Merl uttered a croaking laugh. "Give 'im the boots, Gabe," he said. "But don't stomp him clear under. I owe him plenty. I want a chance to pay off."

Lee put a bullet between Merl's feet. The slug chewed into the hot earth, missing the man's toes by a thin margin. "Move!" Lee said. "You too, Major."

Merl was stampeded into a trot. Mike Bastrop refused to bow to Lee's will to that extent, but he could not resist lengthening his stride as he followed Merl.

Lee waited until the two men were some distance away. They halted and he drove them still farther out in the flat with a bullet close over their heads. They paused, and he sent a final shot as a warning not to return.

He placed his rifle against a bush and shed his pistol and the weapon he had taken from Mike Bastrop, leaving them at a distance.

Gabe Tice hadn't really believed Lee would go through with it. Now a wicked flame blazed in his eyes. He had beefy shoulders, with a stomach that folded just a trifle over his belt. He had greasy hair the color of faded straw and his whiskers grew in patches on a coarse face. He rubbed his palms down the sides of his breeches and then clenched his fists in greedy anticipation.

Lee moved in. He knew that Gabe had experience at roughhouse fighting where a man could bite and kick and gouge and take any unfair advantage. But he also knew his own strength. And this would not be his first try at this sort of conflict.

He knew it would be Gabe's plan to overwhelm him with weight, strength, and ferocity right at the start. Gabe probably would also attempt to plan the battle so that he would be in a position from which he could get to the weapons Lee had set aside.

Gabe came in slowly for a few strides and then erupted with a headlong dive at Lee's knees, intending to bowl them both to the ground where his superior weight would come into play.

Lee had expected something like that. What Gabe encountered was a knee. It was driven into his chin. Teeth were loosened and lips were mashed. Gabe clawed frantically for Lee's legs in an attempt to bring him down, but missed.

Lee caught his man by the hair, lifted his head, and drove a knee again to the face. Gabe joined his brother in misery with a shattered nose.

Gabe's strength told. He managed to clamp both hands on Lee's left arm. He tried for a hammerlock, intending to dislocate the shoulder. Lee twisted, dived forward, carrying Gabe off balance, and broke free.

Gabe sprawled on the ground. He rolled over and over with Lee trailing him. Lee leaped on him, his knees driving into Gabe's stomach. He smashed Gabe in the face with his fists.

Gabe had wanted a fight with no quarter asked, and this was what he was getting. Lee caught him by the hair again, rolled him over, knelt on his back, and jammed his face into the hot earth. "Eat dirt!" he panted. "Eat! And then some more!"

Gabe gagged and choked. Lee hammered his head on the earth. "Eat!" he raged.

He became aware of a frightened voice screaming, "Please! Please! You're killing him! Please stop!"

Clemmy O'Neil was tugging at him, trying to drag him off his victim. He looked at her for seconds before he fully realized who she was. Such was the haze of fury. He had been remembering the agony of the quirt as Gabe had laid on the lash.

Clemmy seemed to be praying. Praying that he would come to his senses.

That shocked him out of his moment of madness. He stopped jamming his victim's head into the earth and got to his feet. He was gasping for breath, retching with the aftermath of the struggle.

Gabe lay dazed, blubbering with pain. His shirt had been torn from his back. "You busted my ribs," Gabe moaned. "You're no human being. You're a devil!"

Lee looked at Clemmy. Her eyes were dark gray in a colorless face. She acted as though she expected she might be the next object of his fury.

He saw that Bastrop and Merl Tice were returning. They were moving hesitantly, as though expecting to be ordered back. Clemmy had a rifle in her hands. She had followed him, against his wishes, and evidently the rifle had made sure that the two men out there would not interfere in the fight.

Lee rounded up the three horses and tied to the saddles the rifles and pistols he had seized. Gabe was sitting up, his face buried in his hands. Blood was flowing and flies were gathering. Gnats began to swarm. Bastrop and Merl Tice were still wary about moving closer.

"He's all yours," Lee called. He had manhandled Gabe with more anger than he had intended, but the man was big and tough and should be able to make it back to safety with the help of his companions.

Clemmy still bore that blanched look. "Maybe you had better head back the same way they're going," Lee said. He motioned toward the horses. "Pick the one you want. No need for you to walk. That's for scum like them."

She shook her head and silently mounted the black horse Bastrop had been riding. Lee swung into the saddle of one of the other mounts.

"You must know what you're doing by this time," he said. "You saw it. That's the way a Comanche would have worked him over. So now we both know for sure."

Still without speaking, she followed him as he rode away. Mike Bastrop shouted after them, "Girl, are you crazy? You'll die in that country. There's no water for eighty miles. Don't stay with that red devil."

Clemmy did not look back, nor answer. Lee presently turned in the saddle. The three men were walking westward across the flat into the setting sun. Gabe Tice seemed able to keep up with his companions without help.

CHAPTER SIX

Leading the three captured horses, they rode through sand dunes whose undulating swells were bathed in a wash of gold by the sun. There was no wind, and the tracks of their animals stretched out in a wide swath behind them.

Lee answered the question in Clemmy's eyes as she looked back. "The wind will spring up tonight. By morning there'll be no sign we came this way."

They left the dunes. Lifeless, barren hills closed in around them. The horses, dispirited these last several miles, seemed to find something to enliven them. They crossed a rincon and descended a narrow canyon that was little more than a slit in the hills.

Willows and green grass began to appear. The defile widened suddenly and they emerged into the open. A band of deer went bounding away.

Clemmy uttered a little surprised cry. A long basin, enclosed by the barren hills, was spread before them. She could see the shimmer of a sizable lake in the purple twilight. Geese and ducks squawked in reedy marshes.

"The Comanches had a long name for this place," Lee said. "It meant The Place Where the Spirits Walk. I've also heard them use a Spanish term for it. *La Ciudad Sombra.* The City of the Ghosts."

She shivered a little. "A fearsome name for such a pretty place," she said. "I've heard stories about a place like this out on the plains. There's a legend among cowboys about a waterhole that only dead men can find. Some riders who made up their own songs, tell about the Spirit Lake that nobody ever reaches."

Lee nodded. "I know. And there's a legend that a wagon train, heading for California during the gold rush, went into the Devil's Garden, led by a Comanche guide, who told them there was a waterhole ahead. Nobody ever heard of them again. The truth is they were massacred here."

"Massacred?"

"I found the remains of burned wagons when I scouted this place two seasons ago. They're scattered over a stretch of ground beyond the lake, along with bones and skulls. I remember that when I came here with Comanche hunting and war parties they never went near that part of the basin."

Clemmy shuddered again. "I assure you that I never will either."

Lee urged the horses ahead. "That goes for me too," he admitted. "We'll camp as far away as possible. Ghosts, I strictly want nothing to do with."

As darkness came they found a pleasant camping place amid willows along a small, rushing stream that fed the lake.

"This water comes from a spring that boils to the surface less than a mile up the basin," Lee explained. "I guess it goes underground again in that marsh below the lake, for there's no sign of water on the plains south of those hills."

"Why is it that only Comanches know about this place?" she asked.

"The hills we just came through look like scores of others that crop out for a hundred miles," Lee said. "Rough, dry, worthless. There's no real reason for anyone to travel the Devil's Garden by the way we came, and any cowboys or explorers who tried it would swing around these hills instead of going through them. That is, if they were in their right minds. I don't think even the Comanches know how they learned about this basin. It is a secret handed down from the old ones."

He added, "White men don't always see what's right before their eyes. For instance, I saw evidence there is plenty of game around this basin. Deer, wild horses, elk, even a few buffalo. I saw fresh sign. Where there's game there must be water."

"I didn't mean it that way," she said. She was sorting through the food supply in order to plan a meal and wasn't looking directly at him.

"Mean what?"

"I didn't mean that you had to be a Comanche to know about this place."

"You still can't have any doubt in your mind, can you?"

"What difference would it make what your blood might be?" she said. "It's what you are that matters."

They dropped the subject. Another matter that they never discussed was the killing of Bill Tice. Since the time Lee had found the empty shells in her pistol a truce had been declared in that respect.

But that did not mean it was forgotten. The questions kept bobbing up in Lee's thoughts. Had she really fired the shots that had taken her uncle's life? And, if she had not, did she really believe that he was the killer?

In her attitude he could find no answer to the puzzles, no hint as to what she was thinking. She evidently had decided to let the matter rest while their more immediate problems were faced.

Circumstances had forced her to share with him the hardships and dangers of living outside the law. She was devastatingly attractive, but theirs could only be an alliance of necessity and nothing more. Between them lay the shadows of two men—the slain Bill Tice and the Comanche chief, Eagle-in-the-Sky, who said he was Lee's father.

After he had cared for the horses, Lee picked up his rifle. "I'll try for a deer while it's still light enough to notch a sight," he said. "They should be watering now. We'll have to get along tonight on what Kink gave us, for any meat I bag will have to cool for a time. Later on, we can have ducks and geese for the taking with clubs."

He answered the question in her eyes. "Don't worry about a fire being seen or a shot being heard. I doubt if there's another human being within seventy miles, excepting, of course, our friends who are hoofing it back to Flat Creek."

He did not have far to hunt. The wild game that came into the basin for water had not learned to fear humans. He dropped a young buck, gutted it, and carried it to camp where he hung the carcass on a limb to cure.

The fire was burning. He heard splashing in the stream. Presently Clemmy returned, dressed and refreshed from a bath.

"That idea stacks up like a thousand dollars' worth of blue chips," Lee said. He found the pool, stripped, and let the cool water drive some of the fatigue out of him.

Rancho Verde, Punchbowl, the Tices and Mike Bastrop seemed far, far in his past. For the moment, at least.

When he returned to camp, Clemmy had smoke-meat sizzling in the skillet and biscuits in the Dutch oven. Grits and canned tomatoes completed the fare.

"I never sat down to a better banquet," Lee said fervently.

"You'll have to get used to it," Clemmy said. "Our larder doesn't offer much variety. Nor much of anything, for that matter."

The saddlebags on the three horses they had taken from Bastrop and the Tices had yielded a meager supply of jerky, tortillas, and coffee, along with an additional skillet and a coffeepot.

"They didn't aim on going too far into the Garden," Lee had commented on the scant rations the trio had carried. "And they didn't intend to bring anybody out with them, I'd say—alive, at least."

Kink had provided tin plates in the pack. They balanced these on their knees as they ate. "I'll fix up some sort of a table and benches tomorrow," Clemmy said. "Later on, I can do a better job when I get rawhide to work with. You'd be surprised what a person can do with rawhide and willow twigs."

"Rawhide? What do you know about working with rawhide?"

"The nuns in the convent at Santa Fe taught us to cook and sew and provide. Maria, my wonderful duenna at the BT, was Mexican-Indian. She taught me to tan hides and make clothes of deerskin. I can even make a moccasin, but that is very hard on the teeth. The best way to soften the leather and weld a watertight sole is to chew them together."

"Squaw work," Lee said.

"Yes, squaw work. Maybe you ought to be thankful I had that training. We might be here for some time."

She began washing the utensils at the stream. "What did the squaws use for soap?" she asked. "And I could welcome a dishpan."

"The same as you're doing," Lee said. "Sand and elbow grease—when they were in the mood to wash dishes at all. As a rule they weren't as particular about it as you seem to be. What else do you need?"

She twisted around, looking up at him. "What do you mean, what else do I need? I need a lot of things."

"We'll soon be out of flour and salt," Lee said. "And coffee too. We can't live always on just venison and wild duck. We need more blankets. More cook pots. And an ax. You could stand some other kind of clothes. Dresses, for instance."

"And just where are you going to get such things? From the ghosts?"

"The same way I intend to get everything else we need."

"Oh!" She added hastily, "I didn't mean to complain. I can get along. I don't need anything. We can make out for quite a while. You know very well they'll be watching all around the plains in case we make it through alive."

"Every place except one, maybe," Lee said.

"Where would that be?"

"The one place they don't expect us. At Punchbowl."

"It's too dangerous, of course," she said.

Lee let the subject drop. But nearly a week later, as she was again scouring the cooking utensils at the stream, he brought in his roan and the buckskin pack animal and began rigging them.

She straightened, the skillet in her hands. "What size dresses do you wear?" he asked, without looking at her. "And boots and shoes? The boots you've got on won't last much longer."

"Dresses? Boots? Where are you going?"

"To Punchbowl to do a little shopping at Sim Quarles' place, like I told you."

"That's crazy! You can't just ride into town and take what you want."

Lee continued saddling the roan. She dropped the skillet and came running. "What—what if you don't come back?" she wailed.

"I'll leave two loaded six-guns and two rifles with you," he said. "And plenty of shells. I'll be gone four, five days. If I'm not back in a week, ride out and get in touch with Kinky Bob, like I told you before."

"I don't need anything," she protested. "Not a thing. I told you before that we can get along."

"You know we can't. We're already about out of everything. We can't live like animals."

"I'm going with you," she said.

She silenced the refusal he tried to voice. "Do you believe I could stay here alone, just waiting? Waiting and worrying! What kind of a person do you think I am? I'd die."

Lee suddenly found a lump in his throat. "Of course," he said. "I should have understood that. I'm sorry. Of course you must go with me. I was thinking that you'd be safer here."

"Safer? Safer?" She shouted it with scorn. "There are things worse than being safe. Haven't you ever been lonely?"

"Yes," Lee said. "I've been lonely."

She hastily began arranging the camp, hanging what little food they had out of reach of animals, covering their other belongings with the tarp.

Lee saddled the black Bastrop horse that she had taken when she fled from the Tice ranch. "One thing's for certain," he commented. "Mike Bastrop's got plenty of good horses, but he sure must be running short of those fancy saddles he has made special for him at San'tone. We've got away with two of 'em already."

He turned the other three horses out. "They'll stay in the basin on graze and water," he said. "That is, unless they decide to join the wild bunch."

They had sighted wild horses once or twice, always at dawn and always far down the basin where they watered and grazed, then retreated to the plains before sunrise. A white stallion with his *manada* of mares had aroused Lee's curiosity, but the glimpses he had of the animal had been too distant and too fleeting for anything more than speculation. He was remembering the big white Barb stallion Mike Bastrop had imported from Spain three years ago which had escaped from the corral at Rancho Verde.

Leading the packhorse, he and Clemmy pulled out before the sun was well up. They followed a different route westward off the plains and reached Flat Creek shortly after midnight. They rested and resumed their journey at noon, heading toward Punchbowl and keeping to cover, avoiding all habitations and blinding their trail as much as possible.

Early darkness had come when the lights of the town appeared ahead. They dismounted in brush along Punchbowl Creek near the outlying structures of the town. Lee helped Clemmy down and steadied her, for she was saddlenumbed after the long miles. "This is as far as you go," he told her. "I'm going in on foot. I'll follow the creek brush into town. You stay right here. Is that a deal?"

"Yes," she said reluctantly. "That is, unless something happens."

"Nothing's going to happen," Lee said. "I've got it all planned. I'll be careful."

"How long will you be gone?"

"No telling. An hour, at least. Longer, most likely. It depends on how late Sim Quarles' stays open."

"You're risking your life just to try to make things easier for me," she said.

"I tell you I'll be back," he said gruffly. He hesitated, then patted her awkwardly on the shoulder. "That's a promise," he said. "I'll be back."

He moved away through the willows. The stream wound into the heart of town between brushy banks. Stars were blazing in the sky when he reached the wooden bridge that spanned the stream at Sumner Street within a block of his objective.

He climbed the bank and chanced a look into the street. Punchbowl was quieting down for the night. The four gambling houses were brightly lighted and busy, but the majority of the stores were closed.

However, Sim Quarles' mercantile, the largest structure in town, was still lighted, as Lee had expected. Sim was always the last to shut his doors to the chance of earning another penny.

Waiting until the way was clear, Lee left the brush and made his way along the rear of buildings toward the mercantile. He paused in a vacant lot on a side street which he had to cross to reach the store.

The mercantile was an unpainted, barny, one-story structure. It had a loading platform at the rear which overlooked a hitch lot where patrons could leave horses and rigs while shopping. The hitch lot was dark and vacant, although sounds indicated there were still patrons in the store.

Footsteps warned that someone was approaching along the side street, and Lee retreated deeper into the lot, crouching down in darkness.

The passer-by loomed up as a vague shadow on the sidewalk. The man suddenly halted. Lee eased his body around so that he could get at his six-shooter in a hurry if need be, for he feared his presence had been discovered.

However, the man merely stood there for second after second. His attention seemed to be fixed on something in Sumner Street. Lee decided the man was entirely unaware of him. The fragrance of bay rum, of good cigar smoke, and of fine whisky came to him. That identified the stroller. Judge Amos Clebe. Those expensive items, whose fragrance always seemed to surround him, were his trademark.

Suddenly the Judge turned. Reversing his course, he walked quickly away down the dark side street in the direction from which he had come. He lived in that direction, in an ornate house on the outskirts of town, and evidently had decided to return home.

Lee waited until sure the street was clear. He emerged, mystified as to what had caused the Judge to change his mind, and peered into Sumner Street. Only three or four establishments were in view at that limited angle on the opposite side of Sumner Street. All were dark except one and that was the ornately painted front of the Silver Bell, which never closed its door.

A ranch wagon and four saddlehorses stood at the hitch rail of the gambling house, for business was always slack at this mid-week hour. Lee recognized one of the horses. It was a sleek sorrel that was in Mike Bastrop's personal string at Rancho Verde. It bore a stock saddle, glaringly new and untarnished.

Lee debated it an instant, wondering why the discovery that Mike Bastrop was in the Silver Bell seemed to be so important to Judge Clebe. Important enough to cause him to change his mind about his own destination, which evidently had been the Silver Bell. Amos Clebe might have wanted to avoid a meeting with the Rancho Verde owner. Or, perhaps, he had forgotten something of importance, and had turned back to his house to get it.

Lee crossed the street and reached the darkness of the hitch lot. He tiptoed up the steps to the loading platform of the store. There was a door for the convenience of patrons and also a wide sliding door that served the storage room. Both were closed, but when he cautiously pressed the thumb latch on the smaller door, the portal opened with scarcely a sound.

A passageway led into the main room. To the left, a door opened into the storage room which was a jumble of packing cases and barrels.

Sim Quarles was waiting on a woman in the dry goods section of the mercantile. The patron was fussily trying to decide on the purchase of material for a dress from the bolts of material the storeman was laying out.

Lee could hear their voices, although they were not in sight at the angle from which he was looking into the main room. He slipped into the unlighted stockroom and waited.

Finally the transaction was completed. He heard the woman leave. The bolt creaked in the street door and all lights except a night lamp were snuffed in the main room. There was a long delay while the storeman carried his cash drawer to his office, counted the day's receipts, and closed the door of the iron safe.

Quarles left by the rear door, which he padlocked on the outside. Lee waited until certain the man was gone, then made his way into the main store.

A supply of gunny sacks was always kept under the counter for the use of riders who were outfitting. Lee helped himself. Keeping below the counter level as much as possible, he snatched items from the shelves. The night lamp gave light enough, but it was also a danger, for he might be discovered by passers-by on the street. The blinds on the street windows had not been lowered.

He tried to take his time until his mental list of necessities was completed. "Soap," he mumbled. "Dishpan, two cook pots. Matches. Let's see. What else?"

He added another slab of bacon from the meat cooler. That stuffed the first gunny sack.

With a second sack, he moved to the dry goods side of the store. He helped himself to a blanket, a quilt, and a rubber tarp. He moved into women's wear. He sorted through a rack of cotton dresses, growing more and more bewildered as to size and style. In desperation he finally stuffed three dresses into the bag. Boots and shoes were another problem, so he finally took three pairs of each, hoping that at least one pair would be within the right size range.

He was so carried away by his success that he left a note on Sim's pad at the cash register which said:

"Charge it to Rancho Verde."

He discovered that the two stuffed gunny sacks would be too much of a load to attempt to spirit out of town. He left by way of the big sliding door which had been bolted from the inside. He left the bundle of clothing beneath the loading platform. Shouldering the other bag, he made his way to the creek brush unseen, and returned to where Clemmy waited.

"For goodness' sake!" she breathed. "You look like Santa Claus."

"I got you the dishpan and soap," he said proudly. "And you haven't seen the half of it. I'll be back with more before you can say pronto."

He returned by his devious route to the mercantile. He was dragging the second bag of booty from its hiding place under the platform when he again heard footsteps approaching the street. He retreated, crabwise, beneath the platform, lowering the gunny sack, and crouched down.

To his dismay, the arrival once more paused in the street. Lee believed he had been discovered. But the man, instead, turned off the street into the hitch lot and halted in darkness at the corner of the loading platform.

Again it was Judge Amos Clebe, redolent of barbershop tonic, tobacco, and whisky. He merely stood there, leaning against the platform in the darkness, little more than an arm's length from where Lee was huddled.

Minutes passed. The judge waited, motionless. More minutes. Lee's nose itched. He did not dare move. His legs began to ache because of his cramped position.

In addition to his discomfort, he was puzzled. There was something in the immobility of the portly figure that held a grimness and a threat. Amos Clebe seemed to be waiting tensely. Lee sensed there was a seething impatience within the man.

More minutes passed. He could hear only occasional activity in Sumner Street. On two occasions, wheeled rigs rattled out of town. A horseman came in off the west trail and entered a saloon down the street. Two riders left town and headed north, talking over their experiences in the fleshpots.

Still, the Judge waited, motionless, silent. A man came down the side street on foot and the Judge retreated deeper into the shadows until the citizen had passed by, evidently homeward bound. Then Amos Clebe returned to his vigil. Lee was sure it was the Silver Bell that held the man's attention. He was remembering that the Silver Bell had seemed to spark some thought of importance in Amos Clebe's mind not many minutes earlier.

He wondered what Clemmy was thinking because of his prolonged absence. And what she might be doing about it. He began doing some wishing on his own account. He wished fervently that she would do nothing.

Amos Clebe moved suddenly. He straightened and took a stride away from the platform. He was outlined against the reflection of light from the Silver Bell.

Lee was startled to see that the Judge had a six-shooter in his hand. It was cocked and he was raising it. There was in his attitude the tautness of a hunter who had waited patiently for his quarry and was now about to make the kill.

Lee heard the scuffle of a horse's hoofs in Sumner Street. Someone had emerged from the Silver Bell and had mounted. He realized that person must be Amos Clebe's target. And that target was, perhaps, Mike Bastrop. Amos Clebe had recognized his horse at the rail of the gambling house and had hurried home to get a weapon in order to assassinate the man everyone believed to be his crony.

This was cold-blooded murder. Instinct caused Lee to intervene. Mainly it was the normal aversion to seeing a human being slain in cold blood. But also there was, deep within Lee, the belief that Mike Bastrop held secrets that were vital to his own life, his own future.

He dived headlong toward the Judge, shouting, "No!" as he moved.

His voice startled Amos Clebe just as he pulled the trigger. The six-shooter roared as Lee's shoulder crashed into Clebe's knees. They both crashed to the ground.

Fear and desperation galvanized the portly Judge. He tore free of Lee's grasp and lurched to his feet. He had clung to the six-shooter and he tried to bring it to bear on Lee, rocking back the hammer.

Lee, on his knees, plunged forward again, taking the

Judge at the knees. The six-shooter exploded almost in his face, but he only felt the sting of the flash and of burning powder. Once again he brought Amos Clebe to the ground. This time he found a grip on the Judge's arm and twisted. Clebe uttered a gasp of pain and was forced to drop the gun.

Lee drove a fist into the Judge's throat and a knee into the man's soft stomach. He felt his victim collapse.

There was shouting in Sumner Street. The voice of Mike Bastrop became audible, rising to a hoarse thunder of fury. "Somebody tried to murder me. I've got a bullet in my arm. I need a doctor before I bleed to death!"

Lee began running. Because a freight shed blocked the rear of the lot, he was forced to use the side street. Confusion gripped Sumner Street. Men were shouting for a doctor. Apparently nobody knew from where the shot had come that had been fired at Bastrop.

Then Amos Clebe began shouting hoarsely, "Stop him! Stop him! This way! It's that Comanche! The one that murdered Bill Tice. He just tried to kill Major Bastrop."

Lee ran desperately. Amos Clebe had recognized him. Men came racing into the side street. A six-shooter opened up. Lee suspected it was Amos Clebe who fired the first shot. He must have found the gun Lee had shaken from his fingers and was emptying the weapon.

A slug tore a long furrow of dust at Lee's feet. Another twitched at his sleeve. He kept thinking, "That gun must be about empty. It must—"

Amos Clebe, however, had one more shell to fire. Lee felt the impact of the bullet. It was as though someone had struck him on the side with a heavy hand. He staggered, reeled ahead, then regained his stride.

He fought for breath. His lungs seemed to be deflated. He could not stop now. Men were pursuing him on foot. He knew that if they overtook him, the chances were they'd hang him on the spot. He kept going.

CHAPTER SEVEN

He was fleeing from the shadow of death, from the faceless violence of a lynch mob. For this was a mob that had now formed. The screeching was that of men who wanted vengeance—and blood.

He felt his strength ebbing. He had instinctively headed for the fringe of town toward where he had left Clemmy and the horses in the thickets along the creek. He veered down a side path. His thoughts were growing as sluggish as his failing strength. He was sure of only one thing. He must not lead them to her. They might take vengeance on her also.

He rounded a shack. A small figure loomed in his path. He tried to swerve away, tried to lift his pistol.

"No! It's me! Clemmy!"

"I told you not to come in here," he mumbled. "Hide! Hide! Quick! They're—"

She was supporting him. "You're hurt!"

The pursuit had hesitated, unable to decide in which direction its quarry had turned in the darkness.

Lee tried to push Clemmy away. "Get out of here!" he said. "Don't let them catch you."

She hurried him along with her. "I've got the horses handy," she said. "I brought them in closer when I heard the shooting start. They're right here. Are you able to ride?"

Lee found a measure of strength returning. He was bleeding, but he hoped he had sustained only a rib glance. He saw the horses in the darkness. Even the buckskin packhorse, with the bulging gunny sack lashed to its saddle, was there.

Men were now moving in their direction, but still uncertain and peering into the darkness. Discovery was only a matter of seconds.

"I'm all right," Lee said. He pushed her toward her mount, waited to make sure she was in the saddle, then pulled himself on his roan. They raced away.

Wild shouts arose. "There they are!" a man screeched. "They got horses! There's more'n one of 'em!"

A pistol opened up. More joined in. "Hold your fire, you danged fools!" an aggrieved voice boomed. "You just busted a window in my own house. Remember, there's innocent folks around here. I've got kids in there sleepin'."

The shooting ended. The pursuers had no horses within quick reach. Lee and Clemmy reached the creek brush north of town and followed it for a time. They were well away from town and swerving into open flats before they heard evidence of riders on their way out of the settlement. But the pursuit was far away, evidently scattered and confused.

Clemmy pulled alongside Lee, peering anxiously at him. "How about it?" she demanded.

Lee had explored his injury. "Only a graze," he said. "Knocked the wind out of me for a minute."

He fought back the desire to groan with pain, for that was what was driving through him. His injury was far more than a scratch. The bullet had glanced. But it had broken a rib, at least, and perhaps two. He was sure, however, that it had not damaged a lung.

His manner deluded Clemmy. "We'll take a look at it in a little while to make sure," she said. "There's a BT windmill tank above Turtle Flat in the direction we're heading. There should be water in it. It'll take half an hour or so to get there. Can you hold out until then?"

Lee said that he could. But he was mighty thankful when the windmill showed against the skyline ahead. He reeled drunkenly when he slid from the saddle.

Clemmy, with a gasp of fright, came with a rush to steady him. She searched his pockets and found his book of matches. She handed them to him. "Are you able to give me some light?"

"Somebody might see us," he protested.

"That's a chance we'll have to take," she said. "Some light, please."

Lee complied, but even that took effort. She pulled off his blood-stiffened shirt. He heard her draw a deep breath.

"Just a graze," she said shakily. "You idiot!"

If the sight of blood and bullet-torn flesh terrified her, she refused to let it give her a pause. There was water in the windmill tank. She used his shirt to clean the wound, then formed a bandage.

She tried to help him into the saddle when they prepared to ride again. He huffily refused assistance.

He managed to pull himself on his horse, but he reeled and was forced to cling to the horn. Clemmy mounted and pulled her horse alongside so that she could place an arm around him to steady him.

His head cleared. The world quit spinning. "Next time," she said huskily, "Don't be so proud. Even a woman can be of some help."

He tried to pull away from her. "What am I?" he mumbled. "A child?"

"Even a child would have brains enough to accept help when it's needed," she snapped. "Don't be a fool."

She stayed close at his side as they headed away, but Lee found a measure of strength returning.

He looked around after a time. "What's this?" he demanded. "If we keep riding in this direction, we'll land at the BT."

"Yes," she said.

"Have you gone loco?"

"The BT might be the last place they'd think of looking for you," she said. "They'll expect you to head back to the plains. Merl and Gabe probably will join in the hunt as soon as they get word. Maybe we could hide in that rabbit warren that Uncle Tice built. There are rooms that haven't been used in years. I know my way around the kitchen and the pantry. We won't starve, and I'm sure they'll never know they have guests."

"Besides," she added, "I still need some clothes, as long as you seem to have bungled the job."

Events had been so crowded that Lee had not been able to sort them out in proper order. Now some of it came back. He began laughing crazily. Clemmy spoke. "Are you all right? Can you hold out a little longer? It's only a couple of miles."

"I haven't gone off my rocker. I was only thinking about what I left lying under the platform at Sim Quarles' store," he said.

"What was it?"

"Well, to mention a few things, there were three of the

most fashionable dresses I could lay my hands on in a hurry."

"Dresses? You didn't really—!"

"And slippers and a new pair of boots. And a few other items to wear that I won't describe."

"I should just think you wouldn't *dare* describe them. The idea, you trying to pick out what I'm to wear!"

She added, "What will people think when they find those things?"

Then they both were laughing. They were a little fey, a trifle lightheaded. "At least you brought a dishpan," she gasped. "But I'm afraid I've already put a dent in it when I threw that gunny sack on the packsaddle."

After a time they sobered. The gaiety faded. Lee became aware of the grinding pain of his wound, of futility, of complete weariness. Clemmy rode slumped in the saddle.

"I heard someone in that mob that was chasing you say you had tried to kill Major Bastrop," she spoke, breaking a long silence. She was picking her words, trying to be casual about it. But he knew it was important.

"Would you believe me if I told you that man was wrong?" he asked.

"Why shouldn't I believe you?"

"You didn't really believe me when I told you I didn't kill Bill Tice. Or pretended not to believe me."

"Pretended? Oh, I see! You're still trying to say that I was the one who shot Uncle Tice. And that I'm trying to hang the guilt on you."

"If you didn't do it, then who did?"

"There you go again!" she exploded. "That's as much as saying I did it. *You* had more reason to do a thing like that. At least Uncle Tice never used a quirt on me."

"Maybe not, but you still might get it unless you simmer down," Lee warned. "Quit screeching before somebody hears you. And ease that horse down before I take the both of you in hand."

"You just try it," she panted. But she lowered her voice and slowed the pace of the horse.

"That's better," Lee said. "Now, tell me something. Why would Judge Clebe try to kill Mike Bastrop?"

She had intended to ignore him, but that brought her around. "What?"

"You heard me."

"You must really be out of your head!" she exclaimed.

"The Judge was the one who took that shot at Mike Bastrop. Winged him in the arm. If I hadn't jumped the Judge he might have punched the Major's ticket for keeps. Then Judge Clebe tried to kill me too. And almost did."

He told her the details. She listened in silence. He took that silence to mean disbelief.

"You think I'm making all this up, don't you?" he demanded. "I know it sounds crazy. Why would the Judge try to drygulch Major Bastrop? He's always been a pompous, soft old windbag. Harmless as butter. He never even packed a gun in his life."

"Maybe he wasn't as soft and harmless as people believe," Clemmy said.

"You got any particular reason for saying that?"

"I told you I used to peek at the poker games they played at BT. And eavesdrop. There was something horrible about it. The danger, I mean. I always felt they'd skin me alive if they caught me. And Uncle Tice nearly did when he finally pounced on me one night."

"What do you mean, horrible about it?"

"Those three men played as though they hated each other," she said. "And it wasn't because of the game. That meant nothing. There was something else between them. The poker game was only an excuse for them to get together. And to divide up money."

"Divide?"

"I saw that happen. Only twice. But I'm sure it happened many times. That was what bound the three of them together. It wasn't poker. It was something bigger than that. Everybody knew that Uncle Tice was a sort of partner of Major Bastrop. I'm sure Judge Clebe was in on it also. Secretly."

"There's no law against being partners in marketing beef," Lee said. "Maybe the Judge, being as he sits on the bench, figured it better to keep it under his hat."

"I don't know what was in his mind," she said, "but, as far as Amos Clebe being a harmless old windbag, that couldn't be farther from the truth. I was deathly afraid of him. He was always looking at me with those wise eyes. I'd rather be watched by a wolf. Also, as for him never carrying a gun, the fact is that he *was* armed. Always. At least when he played poker at BT."

"Amos Clebe? I never saw a gun on him in my life!"

"He carried one of those wicked, little pistols with two barrels, fastened to a metal device up the sleeve of his shirt."

"A double-barreled derringer with a spring clip!" Lee exclaimed. "Good Lord!"

"He also had a horrible dagger in a sort of sheath that hung at the back of his neck."

Lee whistled, amazed. "Throw-knife! Are you sure you're talking about Amos Clebe? How did you find out about these hideouts?"

"One night he shed his coat when they played poker. He said it was because of the heat, but that wasn't the real reason."

"And what was the real reason?"

"I'm sure he wanted them to know he could defend himself. Uncle Tice and Major Bastrop wore weapons, too. Sixshooters in holsters. But they always carried them openly."

"While they were playing poker?"

"Yes. Well, not at first. You see, I started spying on them way back when I was small. It was different then. They actually seemed to be playing a friendly game. Nobody carried weapons. But, as I look back on it now, I can see how the atmosphere changed. Not suddenly. Those three men came slowly to distrust each other. And fear each other. But something bound them together."

"What you're actually saying is that it could have been Judge Clebe or Mike Bastrop who murdered Bill Tice that night."

"Yes," she said.

"At least that explains why Judge Clebe came back a second time to the mercantile. He hurried home to get a heavier gun when he saw that Mike Bastrop was in the Silver Bell. The range was too long for a derringer."

"I know that they hated you, also."

Lee's wound had been taking toll, along with the hours of great physical stress. His mind had been too numbed to try to puzzle out an answer to the problem Clemmy had presented.

But he now straightened, startled. "Me?" he exclaimed. "You mean Bill Tice and the Judge. I always knew Mike

Bastrop had it in for me, but he might have had a reason. But the other two . . ."

"I heard your name mentioned only once," she said. "That was a long time ago. I don't know why it was brought up. It seemed to touch off some sort of a fury in Uncle Tice. He upbraided Major Bastrop. He seemed to be blaming the Major for something he'd failed to do. Judge Clebe got between them, or they might have gone for their guns. Judge Clebe was very angry. I don't know what he told them, but it quieted them down. I never heard them mention you since that night."

At that moment they topped a rise and lights showed far ahead. "There's the BT," Clemmy said.

"We can't hole up there," Lee said.

"Why not?"

"What would we do with the horses? That just occurred to me. We can't just stake them out in the brush. They'd likely be found, sooner or later. And if we turned them loose, it'd be a dead giveaway, for they'd head for their corrals."

"You're right," she said wearily. "I wasn't thinking straight."

"I've got another idea," he said. "As long as we're here, you ought to get what you need in the way of clothes. I'll sneak in with you to sort of take care of any trouble that might crop up. If we're quiet, we might have luck. I didn't have much trouble injuning in that night. It's late. The bunkhouse ought to be asleep, and the Tice brothers, too, if they're home. It looks like word of the ruckus in town hasn't got this far as yet."

"What is this plan?"

"We'll head for Rancho Verde."

"Verde? But I don't see—"

"That's another place they likely won't think of looking for us. I've got a friend there we can trust. Kinky Bob. He's got a shack of his own. He likely can hide the horses for a day or so while we rest up enough to head for the Llano."

He added, "We've got no time to debate it. If we don't make it to Verde before daylight, we're as good as cooked."

"All right," she said. "I'll hurry. I hope you know what you're doing."

They left the horses at a distance and moved in. The huge, rambling house was dark, but as they passed the main wing, they could hear a sleeper snoring.

"That's Merl," Clemmy breathed. "He always snores. Gabe is probably home, too. Dear God, don't let them wake up tonight!"

They crept to the wing where she had lived. The door of her quarters was locked, but one of the windows was open. Lee helped her scramble across the sill. He waited outside until she handed him a bundle wrapped in a quilt and slid over the sill to join him.

"I tried to leave things in place, hoping they won't suspect I've been here," she whispered.

They returned to where they had left the horses and mounted. Clemmy drew a deep breath when they were at a safer distance. "We've been lucky—this far," she said.

It was perilously near daybreak when they again left their horses and warily approached the adobe hut where Kinky Bob lived. Their cautious tapping on the door brought action. Kinky Bob opened the portal a few inches.

"Lawd A'mighty! I knowed it was you, Jack-Lee, when I heard you at de door. An' if'n it ain't Missy Clementine with you. Folks are sayin' dat both o' you must be daid."

Kinky Bob was wrapped in a quilt he had snatched from his pallet. "Git inside!" he breathed, "afore somebody see you. Don't you two know yo're wanted fer murder?"

CHAPTER EIGHT

Kinky Bob led their horses into hiding in thick brush at a distance from the spread. It was a temporary concealment. Dawn was breaking when he came stealing back to the shack.

"Dey'll be safe enough where I picketed 'em today," he said. "Nobody rightly go near dat brush. Tonight I'll move 'em to better cover. I know a few places where dey kin be handy when you need 'em."

"We're only asking you to cover us until we can get some rest," Lee said. "We'll pull out tonight."

"If'n you ask me, Jack-Lee, you don't look like you can do much more ridin' for a few days. You just make up your mind to lay low here 'til things clear up."

Clemmy spoke. "It's too much of a risk for you, Kink. We wouldn't ask you to hide us even for a few hours if we weren't desperate."

Kink pulled aside the pallet that served as his bed and removed a trap door that was fitted so carefully in the plank floor, its existence might have been overlooked.

"Dug myself a root cellar, years ago," he explained. "Dat's why I put in a plank floor in de shack. Used to be a clay floor. Dar's a crawl tunnel out of de root cellar dat you can find if you know where to dig. I mudded up dis end of it. If'n you foller it, you come out under de old hay rack dat's stored in de wagon shed out dar about a rope throw. De openin' in de floor o' de shed is covered by old planks what look like dey been dar fer years."

Kink grinned reassuringly at Clemmy. "Missy, you cain't find a safer place dan right here, now kin you?"

"Why did you build this tunnel, Kink?" she asked.

"I was born a slave, Missy. I don't never want to be one ag'in. I aim to make sure I kin run fer it if'n dey ever come for me."

"They'll never come for you for that again," Clemmy said.

Lee was fighting to stay on his feet. Clemmy saw his

ashen color and uttered a little cry of contrition. "We stand here talking while this man is suffering," she exclaimed.

Kinky Bob had long experience at emergency treatment of broken bones and injuries that were a part of the rough life of cowhands. Caring for bullet wounds was not exactly a novelty for him, either.

With Clemmy's help, he doctored and bandaged Lee's injury. Lee sat, enduring the pain, while they dressed the wound. When it was finished, Clemmy helped him to the pallet. "Sleep now," she said. "You'll be all right soon."

He was adrift for a time on a sea of pain and feverish dreams. Clemmy stayed at his side. Kinky Bob had left to go about his daily task of gentling the rough string in order to avoid arousing suspicion.

"Ain't much chance anybody'll come near de shack," he had assured Clemmy. "Kink don't have any visitors. But, if'n anybody shows up, you'n Jack-Lee kin hide in de root cellar, or git away through de tunnel."

Nobody came near the shack all day. Lee was aware that Clemmy was trying to soothe him, for he was fighting phantoms in his fever. He knew he was babbling wild things in the Comanche tongue and that she was pleading with him to be quiet. At times, reality would return. He would look up at her, knowing he had been raving.

"What was I talking about?" he would ask.

"Nothing that anybody could understand," she would answer. "Sleep now. Sleep." He could see her weariness. He could see her strength. Her determination.

He finally sank into real sleep. When he aroused, darkness had come. His fever was broken. Kink was back in the shack, cooking a meal, with an oil lamp burning. Clemmy lay sleeping on a blanket in a corner, curled in a childlike posture.

Kink put a finger to his lips when he saw that Lee was awake. "Let de missy sleep," he whispered. "She stayed awake all day, 'til I come home."

Lee tried to move. He failed. It seemed to him that minutes passed before he could form words. "Nobody came?"

"Nope," Kink whispered. "But dey's sure lookin' fer you an' de missy. I sighted riders a couple o' times durin' the day, way off on the range in the direction o' the

Armadillos. All de riders in de crew pulled out to join in de hunt. I rode down to the stage road a while ago to talk to a freighter. Pretended I'd run short o' matches for my pipe. Done some talkin'."

"What did you find out?"

"Somebody put a slug in Majah Bastrop's arm last night in Punchbowl. But only a gouge. He'll be all right in a few days. Them kind never die."

"Who do they say did it?" Lee asked.

Kink didn't want to answer that for a time, but finally he did. "Jedge Clebe says he seen you do it."

"He's lying, Kink. You'd never believe me if I told you who really winged the Major."

"De Majah's put a price on yore haid," Kink said.

"A reward? How much?"

"A hundred dollars if yo're brought in alive. Five thousand dead."

Clemmy had awakened. She sat up, wide-eyed. "How terrible!" she cried.

"It's like I tol' you before, Jack-Lee," Kink said. "De Majah want you in yore grave. Who'd bring you in alive, when he could git rich by packin' in a corpse?"

"Nothing adds up," Lee said. "Why would he want me dead?"

Neither Clemmy nor Kink had an answer.

Within twenty-four hours Lee's wound was well on the mend, but he was forced to admit that Kink and Clemmy were right in insisting that he continue to take it easy. However, within another day or two, his restlessness grew as the injury improved.

He and Clemmy could only venture out of the shack at night and after they were sure the ranch was asleep. On the surface, Rancho Verde was resuming a semblance of its normal routine. The Mexican housekeeper and her husband, who cooked and carried on the chores at Casa Bonita, came and went in their duties, but never approached Kink's shack.

Two riders were still on duty, combing the range and taking care of the *remuda,* but four others were still with the posses hunting the fugitives. These four showed up late on the third day. They were unshaven, saddle-stiffened, and tired. They remained only overnight, pulling out the next morning on fresh horses and leading remounts. They were carrying rifles and six-shooters and had a packhorse loaded with food.

"They're still trying to earn that five thousand," Lee commented to Clemmy. "I rode to Kansas and back with those cowhands. Now they want my scalp."

"How long will they keep looking for us?"

"No telling," Lee said. Mike Bastrop had not returned to the ranch. Kink, who continued his normal daily work with the young horses, talked to the two men of the riding crew and picked up information.

"De Majah's ridin' with the posses, his arm in a sling," Kink reported. "He's called off the late beef drive. Won't be no horses needed, but I ain't got orders yet to quit shapin' them up, so I keep workin'. Everybody in dis part o' New Mexico is too busy tryin' to git rich by killin' a man to 'tend to de cattle business."

"You always been quite a lady's man, Kink," Lee observed. "Do you happen to be acquainted with that pretty girl that keeps house for Judge Clebe in Punchbowl?"

Kink grinned, flattered. "You know danged well I been courtin' Celia for a long time. What you drivin' at, Jack-Lee?"

"You need some supplies in town, Kink," Lee said. "Tobacco, or horseshoe nails, or such. It'd do you good to take the day off and see the sights. And call on Celia. I wonder if Judge Clebe is still holding court. And I'm concerned about his health. The Judge was looking poorly the last time I saw him."

Kink eyed him. "I reckon dat won't take much doin'," he said.

He rode away the following morning and did not return until long after midnight. "Ain't no trials bein' held," he reported. "Court is 'journed 'til de Judge gits back from El Paso. He was called dar on important business."

Lee and Clemmy looked at each other. "We might not be the only ones that are running scared," Lee commented.

Kink said the manhunt was still on, but it was beginning to slow down. "Town's full o' riders nursin' saddle blisters," he said. "A lot of 'em figure you two are daid out beyond de Caprock. Either dat or you've made it into Mexico. A lot of 'em are goin' back to their outfits."

"What about Merl and Gabe Tice?" Clemmy asked.

"Celia says she guesses if it wasn't fer dem two rascals

an' Majah Bastrop dar wouldn't be anybody but maybe a few lawmen still out in de brush. I heard say dat de Tices swore on their father's grave dat dey'd git you, Jack-Lee, an' roast you over a slow fire."

In addition to news, Kink brought Lee a clean shirt and underwear and three pairs of socks. "Me'n de Judge wear about de same size shirt," Kink explained. "He got so many clothes he never miss what Celia give me. I reckon you kin use some of 'em, even if they ain't quite as snug as what you like."

When Kink prepared to leave the shack for his day's chore at the horse pasture the next morning, Lee said, "We'll pull out tonight, Kink. Can you bring in the horses for us?"

"Where'll you an' the missy go?" he asked mournfully.

"We've got a place. It's better that you don't know."

"You mean dey might try to squeeze it out'n me? I reckon dey would if they ketched on dat you'd been here, but I tell you now dey'd never git it out o' me."

"I know that."

"Ol' Kink hankers to go with you an' de missy."

"For your own sake I can't let you do anything like that," Lee said. "Let's face it. You know that the chances are against us. Anybody who is with us will be given the same treatment if they catch us."

"I still hanker to go."

"Kink," Lee said abruptly, "you know I'm Comanche, don't you?"

Kink was taken by surprise. "I don't know nothin'," he exclaimed fearfully. "If you Comanche, if you Mexican, if you white, what difference. We friends."

"You know something," Lee insisted. "Something you've kept from me. You're sure I'm Comanche. Why?"

Kink refused to answer. He picked up his chaps and the bucking strap he used in riding the young horses and left the shack. Peering from a corner of the window, Lee watched him stride to the corral, rope out his day horse, and head for the horse pasture.

"He knows," Lee said. "He knows for sure."

The morning dragged by as had the other mornings since their confinement in the shack.

"You're not!" Clemmy spoke sharply, breaking a long silence.

"Not what?"

"What you said a while ago. Comanche."

"I feel that Kink is sure that—"

"He's wrong. And do you know what else I think? I'm sure you're the baby the Indians stole the day they hit this place. I think that the Señora Margarita Calvin, the widow of John Calvin, was your mother and that John Calvin was your father."

"If so, it'll never be proved," Lee said. "They're dead. How could you prove anything after so many years?"

She stamped her foot. "I tell you there's no Comanche blood in you. Spanish, yes, but very little even of that. Your mother was a Lopez before she married John Calvin, but Americans had married into the Lopez family for generations. Her mother was an American, and so was her grandmother."

"How do you know all this?"

"Maria, my duenna, had a tongue that swung like a bell clapper. She knew all about everyone in the Punchbowl. I could tell you considerable. You'd be surprised at some of the things."

"I'll bet that more than one reputation has been ruined by Maria. But what does all this add up to?"

"You're deliberately pretending to be dense, just to get my temper up," she said. "John Calvin's widow owned all of Rancho Verde. It was part of the original Spanish grant. The Lopez grant, one of the biggest in New Mexico. Now, do you see what I'm driving at? Or do I have to draw a picture and push your stupid nose into it so you can understand that—"

The door of the shack was flung abruptly open. Days of monotony had lulled them into carelessness. They had failed to bar the opening.

Lee whirled. He had been standing near the wall to the left of the door. The intruder who came leaping into the room was Gabe Tice. His beefy face still bore the blotches and healing wounds of the punishment he had taken at Lee's hands. He had a six-shooter in his hand. However, he was momentarily at a disadvantage, for his eyes were fixed on Clemmy. She shrank back, terrified.

Gabe's puffy eyes darted around the room in search of Lee. Lee was already leaping. He brought his left hand smashing down on Gabe's right arm. The pistol fell to the floor. His right fist drove into Gabe's stomach. It was a paralyzing blow. Even so, Gabe tried to retrieve the gun.

Clemmy darted in and snatched up the weapon. Another man loomed in the doorway. Merl Tice. He had a brace of six-shooters in his hands, but he could not fire because of the danger to his brother.

Lee caught Gabe by the waist and propelled him bodily into Merl. The brothers were driven through the door and sprawled on the ground outside.

Lee also fell to his hands and knees. He glimpsed at least two more armed men who were running from the corner of the bunkhouse toward the shack to help the Tices. He recognized them as BT riders.

Clemmy slammed the door shut an instant before a bullet smashed into one of its planks. The shot had been fired by the oncoming BT men.

The two strong wooden bars that Kink used to secure the door stood in a corner. Lee jammed them into place. More bullets beat at the portal, but none of the slugs penetrated the heavy oak planks which had been wedged together with wooden dowels by Kink, who evidently had defense in mind in every detail of his reconstruction of the shack. The walls were of adobe, eighteen inches thick. Only the door, and the three windows, which also had heavy wooden shutters, were at all vulnerable.

Lee pushed Clemmy forcibly to the floor. "Stay down!" he warned as he barred the window shutters.

The shutters were equipped with loopholes. Lee chanced a look. Merl and Gabe Tice were running toward the wagon shed. That offered the nearest shelter. The shed, in which Kink said his tunnel emerged, stood a short distance southwest of the shack. Gabe was doubled over, the wind still knocked out of him by Lee's violence, unable to keep the pace his brother was setting. But Merl kept going.

Lee could have picked off both brothers, but he let them reach cover in the shed, whose crooked double doors stood open, facing north. The two cowboys were doing the shooting. They had halted beyond the wagon shed and were crouched, emptying their weapons.

Lee heard the hammers click on spent shells. He pushed the muzzle of his gun over the ledge of the window and fired one shot. The bullet tore dust between the pair.

"Start running!" he shouted.

They obeyed. One lost his hat in his haste to make it back to the safety of the corner of the bunkhouse. By that time Merl and Gabe Tice had reached the shelter of the shed.

There was a moment of silence. Then Merl Tice shouted, "Come out o' there, you damned copperhide! We've got you dead to rights this time. Come out, or we'll smoke you out an' that featherheaded girl along with you."

Lee looked at Clemmy. "You ought to get out of this."

"And you're going to stay, of course?" she snapped.

"I'm not giving up to those two, at least," he said.

"That makes a pair of us featherheads. What do you think would happen to either of us in their filthy hands?"

Merl Tice opened up with a six-shooter. He screeched profanity and threats as he fired. The slugs died in the heavy adobe walls.

"If we can hold out until dark, maybe we can fool them," Clemmy said shakily. "Remember what Kink said about his tunnel?"

"I remember," Lee said. "Does that still make me a featherhead?"

"That remains to be seen." She picked up a rifle and moved to a window. The west window covered the wagon shed and bunkhouse. A rambling barn also stood in that direction, south of the bunkhouse. The door of the adobe shack stood in the west wall, overlooking these buildings.

The south window faced toward the irrigation ditch and hayfields. The main house was some distance to the northeast, and there was little cover for attackers from that direction.

Lee saw the frightened faces of the Mexican housekeeper and her husband peering from windows in the main house.

More bullets pounded futilely at the shack, coming from windows in the bunkhouse where the two BT riders had posted themselves.

"Quit wastin' caps," Gabe Tice shouted from the wagon shed. He addressed the shack. "You ain't got a chance, Jackson, an' you know it. We'll send for some more men an' we can hold you there 'til you an' the gal starve.

Might as well make it easy on yourself by comin' out now."

For answer, Lee put a rifle bullet through the flimsy plank wall of the wagon shed. He could hear the Tice brothers scrambling around, hurriedly arranging bulwarks to protect themselves. Lee was familiar with the interior of the shed. He had a sinking feeling. If the Tices happened to discover the entrance to Kink's tunnel, any hope of escaping from this trap was ended.

He could see that Clemmy was entertaining the same fear. They waited. Merl Tice was talking to the men in the bunkhouse, but Lee could not make out the words.

However he began to breathe a trifle easier. There was no indication the tunnel had been found. If there really was a tunnel! The thought came that perhaps there never had been one. It might have been only an invention of Kink's imagination in order to give him a sense of security, so that he would remain in the shack until he had recovered his strength.

Silence came for a time. Then they heard a horse leaving the ranch. The rider was one of the BT cowboys who had retreated to where they had left their mounts. The man kept buildings between himself and the adobe shack until he was out of range, then headed north in the direction of Punchbowl.

"How do you suppose they found out we were here?" Clemmy murmured.

"I should have known they'd get around to suspecting Kink sooner or later," Lee said. "Another thing, I should have seen to it that the door was barred."

Gabe Tice confirmed Lee's surmise a few minutes later. "We'll make that black traitor sorry he was ever born when we get our hands on him," Gabe shouted, breaking the lull. "I should have guessed right from the start he was hidin' you here. You two have always been mighty friendly."

"At least that gives some hope for Kink," Lee said. "They haven't got him—yet. Let's hope he's heard the gunfire and knows what it means, and that he's had sense enough to pile a horse and head for Mexico."

Silence came again. Both Lee and Clemmy knew that the cowboy who had ridden away had been sent to bring reinforcements.

CHAPTER NINE

Hours passed. Late afternoon came, with the sun blazing down. The heavy dirt roof, on which bluebonnets and wild sunflowers bloomed, and the thick adobe walls insulated the interior of the shack. The room remained fairly cool.

However, the wagon shed, which had no windows, evidently was a furnace. Its double doors stood open, facing to the north, but this was of no help to the Tice brothers because the breeze was not drawing from that direction.

Lee heard them smashing a way of escape through the west wall. He sent a bullet into the shed, but aimed high, for he had no desire to kill—not even the Tice brothers. He wanted to help drive them from the shed. He was answered by bullets that beat at the heavy window shutters, bullets that sought his life.

He withdrew from the window. He pulled aside the pallet and lifted the trap door to the root cellar. "I hope Kink wasn't dreaming when he said he'd dug a burrow out of here," he said. "It's time to find out."

He descended the short ladder into the excavation. The space was so low he had to duck his head to avoid the beams that supported the plank floor. He could almost span the width and length of the cellar with his outstretched arms. The last of Kink's potato supply lay in a barrel, adorned with long sprouts. A supply of jerked beef that was as hard as leather, a bag of black-eyed beans, and another of cornmeal, along with a few cans of vegetables, rounded out Kink's cellar larder. However, Kink had said that he had a larger food cache hidden out somewhere. Kink's main purpose in life seemed to be to make sure he could get away "when they came for him."

At his request Clemmy handed down the lamp and matches. He lighted the wick. He could hear her moving from window to window, keeping watch. He explored the walls with his hands, but the earth seemed solid.

Clemmy gave him the stove poker, with which he began

probing the west face of the cellar. That got results. The poker pierced deeply into softer earth. Lee widened the opening until he could thrust his arm into it at full length. His fingers touched nothing.

He doused the lamp and climbed back into the room. "I found it," he said. "Kink closed it up with small rocks and plastered it with wet clay. There's no use opening it entirely until we're sure there's no other way. We've got to hang on until dark. Then we will have a chance, at least."

He saw her swallow hard. "That ground looks solid enough," he said reassuringly. "Kink knows it's safe."

"I'm not afraid," she said. Then she drew a deep breath and tried to force a smile. That failed. "That's a fib," she said. "I *am* afraid. I've always been afraid of dark places, tunnels and such. I've had nightmares about being trapped in caves."

"We won't have any trouble," Lee said. "Kink built it. He's almost as big as both of us put together."

"Of course," she said.

"Maybe Gabe and Merl will give it up as useless," he said. It was a lame thought and he knew it.

"Maybe we can wish them away," she said.

"Wish them away?"

She again tried to smile wanly. "It's a game I used to play as a child. Well, not always as a child. I still wish for things. I used to wish that Merl and Gabe would vanish. I would sit by the hour, just wishing."

"Did you ever win?"

"Oh, yes. Not as far as Merl and Gabe were concerned, of course. Sometimes things turned out the way I wished."

"What, for instance?"

Color suddenly rose in her throat and she wouldn't look at him. "Oh, it doesn't matter. It was just a lot of foolishness. To pass time. I've always been left to my own devices. Maria, my duenna, was about the only person I ever knew whom I could confide in, or go to for advice. But Uncle Tice sent her away after I became old enough to look after myself."

"You never knew your mother?"

"I remember a beautiful woman who came to the convent and held me tight in her arms. A woman who kissed me and told me how much she loved me and that very soon we would be together always. She said she was

earning money enough so that we could go somewh
and live comfortably. She mentioned San Francisco."

Tears were glistening in her eyes. "Yes, I knew
mother. She was good. She was an actress, but t
doesn't mean that the things evil-minded people say w
true. It's only that most women were jealous of
because she was so beautiful, so talented. It was
tongues of women that crucified Rose O'Neil. Women
so cruel to women."

"And they haven't changed," Lee said. "They've
another Rose O'Neil to crucify because she's young a
pretty and is everything they wish they were deep in th
hearts."

She looked at him through swimming eyes, surpris
"Thank you for the pretty part of it, even though you
only trying to cheer me up. They've hurt me. I woul
ever want them to know that. They have, but I'll ne
kneel to them. That's all they want. To humble me,
they can patronize me."

A bullet smashed into the door, breaking a long
Lee moved to a peephole. Powder smoke was fading
the hot sunlight from where a rifle had been fired fron
knothole in the weathered side of the barn beyond
bunkhouse.

Gabe Tice's heavy voice rose tauntingly. "That's just
let you know we're still around, Comanch'. No use tr
to wriggle away toward Casa Bonita. Ken Burns is hu
ered in the barn, an' he's got all that stretch o' gro
covered. You know Ken. An' you know he can sh
straight."

Merl took up the theme. "We're askin' you once m
to come out peaceful. Clemmy, why did you pick up v
an Indian? We're goin' to blast him out o' there ri
soon. You might git hurt."

"Start blasting," Clemmy responded.

Gabe cursed her. She clapped her hands over her e
Gabe finally fell silent. No more shots were fired.

"Don't get careless," Lee warned her. "They're gett
anxious. It's almost sundown, and nobody's showed up
help them."

He peered from a loophole. A bullet struck within
inches of the opening.

"They've got the loopholes spotted," he said. "Don't linger at one, like I just did, for more than a quick look. If that fellow had been a better shot, I'd have got that .44-40 right between the eyes."

The north window gave them a view of the trail to Punchbowl. It had remained empty since the messenger had vanished in the direction of town hours earlier.

Lee looked at the sun which was now touching the rims of the buttes to the west. "Won't you ever go down?" he blurted out.

He returned to the north window after a time to watch the trail. He remained there so long, Clemmy joined him. They both gazed in silence.

Riders were approaching on the trail. They were still nearly a mile away, but the setting sun caught the glint of rifle steel.

The trail carried the horsemen out of sight into timber. After a time they reappeared, much closer.

"Six, seven, eight!" Lee murmured, counting. "With the Tices, we're up against ten, eleven men, at least."

The sun went down at last. The sky darkened. The riders had left the trail and circled to a point beyond the buildings where their approach would be covered by the barn and the bunkhouse.

Lee and Clemmy waited. They could visualize what was going on. The arrivals would have left their horses at a distance and moved in on foot to confer with the Tice brothers as to the strategy they would follow.

Twilight lingered. Clouds became masses of gold. The weathered shakes on the buildings were the hue of hammered copper. Their splintery plank walls became a rich russet shade.

Lee speculated on Mike Bastrop's whereabouts. He had recognized the majority of the reinforcements. Sheriff Fred Mack had been leading the group, but Bastrop had not been present. Evidently the Rancho Verde owner was still out in the range, seeking trace of the fugitives elsewhere.

He felt Clemmy's shoulder touch his arm. She had moved close to his side. There was now no shadow of doubt between them. He no longer entertained the slightest belief that she had slain Bill Tice. He was certain also that she no longer suspected he might have been Tice's killer. In fact, he felt that she had never really believed it from the first.

A voice began shouting in the barn. "This is Sheriff Mack speaking. Can you hear me, you two in the shack?"

Lee delayed his reply for seconds. He was playing for time. That was their only ally. Darkness was their only hope.

"I can hear you," he finally responded.

That brought a stir of boots and a subdued rumble of voices. Men were stationed in the barn and bunkhouse. Others, no doubt, were spotted along the irrigation ditch to prevent escape in other directions.

"Come out, unarmed, with your hands up," the sheriff yelled. "In the name of the law."

"And be shot full of holes in the name of the law," Lee answered.

"You'll be taken to town with the privilege of facin' a trial, fair an' square," Fred Mack said.

Lee was certain the officer was making a promise he knew he could not keep. He was asking a man to show himself so that he would likely be shot down or seized and hanged.

Lee remained silent. He kept watching the sky. Deep shadows were forming in the draws on the flanks of the Armadillos. The range below was fading into a sea of mauve light.

"Are you comin' out, or do we come in an' drag you out by the heels?" Merl Tice shouted, infuriated.

Lee spoke to Clemmy. "Take the poker and the lamp. Go down and open that tunnel. Don't light the lamp until I cover the trap. Here are the matches. We can't let any light show. They'll rush us as soon as it gets dark. We've got to be gone before they shoot down that door. Douse the lamp the minute you've got the tunnel open."

She complied. She was pale, but calm. She had the presence of mind to take with her into the root cellar the bundle of garments she had brought from her room at BT.

Lee replaced the trap door and shoved the pallet over it to mask any trickle of lamplight that might betray their plan.

"If you're any kind of a man," Fred Mack shouted,

"you'll let that girl come out. We don't aim to hurt even such as her."

Clemmy heard that. "Tell them that such as I will put a bullet in the rotten hide of the first one that tries to rush this place," she said, her voice muffled.

Lee didn't relay the message. He was still buying time. He could hear the rasp of quarreling voices. The officer was engaged in a dispute with the brothers. Lee got the gist of it. Fred Mack was hesitating about leading an assignment where a girl's life might be at stake. The Tice brothers were furiously demanding action and denouncing him as a coward.

The Tices prevailed. A six-shooter opened up. Other pistols and rifles joined in. A storm of bullets smashed savagely at the door. The roar of guns went on and on. It was plain that the posse had a definite plan, and also had the ammunition to see it through.

Slugs began to chew through the planks. Lee heard spent bullets buzzing in the room. Some were coming through with such force they buried in the opposite wall. The door could not sustain that torrent of metal much longer. The upper hinge was torn from its supports.

"I've opened the tunnel!" Clemmy spoke during a brief lull in the uproar.

Lee said, "Put out the lamp." He pulled aside the pallet, lifted the trap door and passed down rifles and ammunition.

He moved to the west window, his rifle loaded. Gunfire spurted from the barn and bunkhouse, but there was no indication that the wagon shed had been reoccupied.

A new rain of slugs beat at the door. It began to sag, and yells of triumph arose from the posse.

Lee lifted his rifle and emptied it at the bunkhouse and barn. He spaced his bullets along the length of the structures. That slowed the shooting as men scrambled for cover.

He reloaded, making sure they could hear the metallic click of the mechanism. Again he emptied the rifle. He was seeking only to make them cautious, to delay the inevitable final attack.

He dropped into the cellar, reached up, and slid the trap door back in place.

"The tunnel isn't very big," Clemmy said in the darkness. Her voice was quivering.

"We've got to try it," Lee said. "Where is the blasted thing? I'm turned around."

She guided him to a wall. His groping hands found the opening. "All right," he said. "I'll go first and take the two rifles."

He crawled into the opening, pushing the weapons ahead of him. "It's plenty big enough," he said. "Come on."

He heard her following him. The tunnel was braced with lengths of cottonwood or mesquite. "Kink did a good job," he whispered. "He's got enough timbering in here to hold up a mountain."

"I hope so," she quavered. "Don't go so fast. Don't get too far ahead of me."

The depth of earth dimmed sounds from above, but Lee could still hear the faint thud of bullets smashing at the door of the shack.

His head collided with a solid object. This time it was not one of the braces. It was a wall of unyielding earth that blocked the way.

He felt freezing despair. "Stop!" he breathed.

"What's wrong?" Clemmy chattered.

Lee did not answer. His first thought was that the tunnel ahead had collapsed. If so, all they could do would be to retreat to the root cellar.

The blackness was so impenetrable it seemed to have substance. Lee found himself fighting panic. If the tunnel had collapsed ahead, it might also cave in behind them. Or upon them. He could hear Clemmy breathing fast. She spoke again, her voice high-pitched. "What is it?"

Lee groped in the darkness. His hands met only hard rough walls of earth on either side. He explored overhead. He touched nothing. And he could now distinctly hear the roar of guns that were being fired in the bunkhouse and barn.

Suddenly, he stood erect, feeling his knees quivering. His head touched wood. Wooden planks!

He suddenly wanted to yell, but managed to suppress that to a mumble. "Of course! Why, we're there! We've reached the end of the tunnel. I didn't realize we'd crawled that far. I'm standing almost straight and there are planks overhead. We must be under the wagon shed!"

Clemmy began babbling unintelligibly. He placed the palms of his hands against the obstruction and pushed cautiously. At first there was no result. He used more force, and one of the planks yielded. Any sound it made was lost in the roar of gunfire—now startlingly loud. He could see the flickering glow of the explosions, for the double doors of the shed still stood open, although facing at right angles to the buildings where the guns were flaming.

He wriggled out of the excavation and found himself beneath the spidery outlines of the hay wagon. "Give me your hand," he said. "And watch your head. We're coming out right under the hay rick."

He lifted her to the surface. She lay beside him, clinging to his hand like a terrified child. She was sobbing. He placed an arm around her, holding her tight against him until she calmed.

"I'm all right now," she breathed huskily. "I'm sorry I'm such a weakling. Afraid of the dark. I—"

The roar of guns reached a crescendo. Wild yelling swelled up. Lee moved to the open door and peered out. Clemmy joined him. The adobe shack was lighted by the crimson flash of gunfire. Its door was tilted drunkenly, its hinges torn away by the storm of metal.

Fred Mack's voice shouted, "Quit shootin' for a minute! Maybe the cuss is ready to come out now."

The gunfire tapered off. The officer shouted a demand for Lee's surrender. Silence came.

"I'm sick o' stallin' around!" Gabe Tice roared. "Come on, such of you as ain't made of jelly. Me an' Merl are goin' in there an' dig him out."

Guns were reloaded and the firing was resumed. Fred Mack continued to shout for Lee to give up, but his voice was lost in the uproar. Gabe and Merl Tice were shouting orders, organizing the others for a rush.

Lee and Clemmy retreated from the door of the shed. "Here they come!" Lee breathed.

The posse had left cover and were running toward the shack, spreading out to engulf it from three sides. They were shooting as they charged.

Men, crouching and zigzagging, ran past the open door of the shed. One paused, taking shelter back of one of the sagging doors for a time. He had two six-shooters in his hands, and was firing like a madman. Then he charged ahead again, but he was now in the rear of the rush. Lee recognized him. He was Gabe Tice. Gabe was letting other men go in ahead of him.

Lee said, "Let's go!"

The wave of attackers had gone past and their attention was concentrated on the adobe shack. "Stay close to me!" Lee said.

He had his rifle in his hands. He almost fired into a shadow that darted suddenly into the shed through the open door.

"Dat you, Jack-Lee?" a deep whisper sounded. "You dar with de missy?"

Lee felt ice in his veins. He had come within an ace of shooting Kinky Bob. "I'm here, Kink!" he breathed. "Miss Clemmy's with me."

"Praise de Lawd!" the big man said. "I been layin' out dar all afternoon, prayin' you'd hold out 'til dark. Couldn't do nothin' but wait a chance to come in. I follered right behind dem men when dey started to rush my place."

His heavy hand touched Lee's arm. "Let's git out o' here afore dey find de tunnel an' ketch on that you two has got away. The horses are waitin'. It's about a mile away."

The shooting and screeching was at its height around the shack. Someone chanced entering the structure and began bawling a frantic plea for his companions to quit shooting.

Lee and Clemmy followed Kink as they darted out of the shed. They veered until they had its bulk between them and the shack. They headed away and passed the bunkhouse and barn. They were not challenged. All members of the posse apparently had joined in the attack on Kink's adobe stronghold.

Confused shouting arose back of them. It was dawning on the attackers that the bag was empty. Angry accusations were flying. The Tice brothers were frenziedly berating Fred Mack and others for carelessness, accusing them of letting their quarry slip past them in the darkness. This was being angrily denied.

"Dey'll find the tunnel pretty soon," Kink panted as they broke into a run. "But dey'll have plenty trouble pickin' up our trail in de dark. Come daybreak, we be long gone."

The shouting became fainter in the distance. Kink slowed the pace. Weight and age were telling on him. "I never was very light on my feet," he admitted.

Lee was also happy for a respite. Clemmy, realizing they were safe for the time being, said faintly, "I'm bushed!"

She was reeling, exhausted. Lee discovered that, in spite of everything, she had brought with her the bundle of clothing, which she clung to tightly. He lifted her in his arms and carried her, bundle and all.

After a time, she strengthened. "I can travel on my own feet now," she said. "I'm being a baby again."

Kink led the way through brush. Presently, Lee heard the stir of tethered animals ahead. There were seven horses in all, three of which bore saddles. One of them was the buckskin packhorse, bearing a sizable burden.

"I lifted my cache o' grub," Kink said. "I helped myself to some o' de Majah's best ridin' stock—such as you two ain't already got away with. We'll need remounts. It's quite a fur piece to Mexico, so dey tell me, an' we got to git there in a hurry, fer they'll be after us."

"You better head for Mexico alone, Kink," Lee said.

"What you mean, Jack-Lee? Don't you want to ride with me?"

"If you were caught with me, it'd only go harder on you."

Kink laughed scornfully. "How you talk! Dar ain't nothin' dat would help Kinky Bob now, if'n he was caught. Dey would hang me for stealin' horses, if nothin' else. Dey know it was me that kept you an' de missy hid out at my place while dey was ridin' dar horses down to skin an' bones huntin' you."

He added, "I cain't go back, but if you don't want me to travel with you, I'll haul out on my own."

"You know better than that," Lee said. "But I'm not going to Mexico. Not yet, at least."

"Whar you go, Jack-Lee?"

"Into the plains. Into the Garden."

"De Debbil's Garden? Nobody go dar, Jack-Lee! De imp-ghosts git you! Dey ride on de sandstorms!"

Clemmy spoke. "I've been there. No imp-ghosts better come around me. I'll tweak their noses for them."

"Don't talk like dat, Missy," Kink begged. " hoodoos, dey'll hear you."

"We're going into the Garden," Clemmy said, "a you're going with us. You'll be better off with us th alone. They might catch you before you could make it Mexico. We could never forgive ourselves if that h pened."

"Of course," Lee said. He slapped Kink on the ba "That makes three of us now. Mavericks. Outlaws!"

"I got a hoot owl charm that I bought from a wi doctor," Kink said. "An' magic powder to sprinkle on fire at night to keep de hoodoos away. I ain't skeered go to Spirit Lake with you an' de missy, Jack-Lee."

"Spirit Lake?" Lee asked quickly. "You know ab it?"

"Nobody know where 'tis," Kink said, "but I 'spect y think you do. Dar's no such place, but if'n you believe y kin find it, Kink will go along. But I ain't goin' to like None whatever."

They rode eastward. Back of them, distance erased sounds. If they were being hunted, there was no sign their pursuers. They veered northward to set up a bli trail, then headed again directly for the Devil's Garden.

CHAPTER TEN

Dawn was bright on the ridges when they rode out of the arid wastes of the Devil's Garden into view of the green basin. Spirit Lake lay still and gleaming, reflecting the glow in the sky.

Kink pulled up his dust-caked horse and stared for a long time. "De Lawd watch over us all," he finally said. "Dis here is a place dat ain't supposed to be."

His awe increased as they moved toward the camp site in the willows that Lee and Clemmy had used previously. A band of antelope went hop-scotching ahead of them, pausing at intervals to peer at them, and then take off again. Deer moved in the distance. Water fowl squabbled in the reeds.

The horses Lee had turned loose when he and Clemmy had left for Punchbowl had not joined the wild bunch. He sighted them grazing not far away.

However, he stood up in the stirrups, then sank back. "Hold up!" he said. "There are wild horses down the basin, but so far away they likely won't spot us if we stay still. They're starting to pull out for the day."

The wild ones were mere specks at that distance. Among them was a band of mares which was now being herded eastward toward low hills beyond which lay the open plains. Their master was a white stallion. Lee watched until the stallion and his *manada* had vanished into the hills.

The other bands of mustangs, having had their fill of water and grass, retreated to the hills also for the day.

"Remember that big white Barb stud that Mike Bastrop imported from Spain a few years ago, Kink?" Lee asked. "He offered a thousand dollars to anybody who would bring in that stallion. Do you suppose . . . ?"

He let it stand unfinished. Kink drew from inside his shirt a wrinkled object that was attached to a silver chain.

"Don't let de hoodoos fool you, Jack-Lee," he im-

plored. "Dat's one o' dem ghost-devils in de shape of
horse."

"If it's a ghost-devil, it just might be the ghost of t
Barb," Lee said. "There was no way of being sure at th
distance. It likely will turn out to be a tough c
broomtail. But I want a closer look at first chance."

They camped, and watched Kink sprinkle powder fro
a green glass vial onto the fire. The powder burned wi
an ugly purple flame and sent up a puff of pungent smok

"No ghost-devil will hurt us tonight," Kink said.

"I'm afraid the witch doctor who sold that voodo
charm to Kink wasn't exactly honest," Clemmy whisper
to Lee. "Kink thinks it's the foot of an owl that was sh
by a silver bullet in the light of a full moon. It looks mo
like the claw of a Plymouth Rock rooster to me."

But they all slept in peace that night. No ghost-dev
came to hoodoo them.

Lee and Clemmy spent the major part of the next tw
days sleeping. It was the toll they paid for so many da
of tension. Kink let them eat and sleep and sleep and ea
He mumbled over his hoodoo charm, sprinkled powder c
the fire, and remained alert for sign of flesh-and-bloc
intruders.

Lee was beset by many questions, but there was or
above all, for which he had no answer. What of th
future? They had escaped to a domain of their own whe
they could exist indefinitely, if necessary. For months,
least. Even for years, perhaps.

But that was unthinkable. There was water and gam
here. The outside world could be raided for other neces
ties. But there was also loneliness here that would gro
with the passing of time.

They were fugitives. Outlaws! A murder charge w
never canceled by time. Even worse in some ways, esp
cially for a girl, they were outcasts—unwanted by socie

Lee kept thinking of the relentless hatred the Ti
brothers seemed to hold toward him. It went beyond t
bitterness that sons might naturally show toward a ma
they believed had murdered their father. In fact, L
doubted that the brothers had held the great affection f
their father that they now proclaimed. Nor for ea
other, for that matter.

Then there was Mike Bastrop. His animosity seem

even greater than that of the Tices. The five thousand dollars he had offered for Lee's death seemed bloodthirsty beyond all bounds of reason.

Also puzzling Lee was the mystery of Judge Amos Clebe's attempt to ambush Mike Bastrop. He had never given much thought to the corpulent, pompous Judge. To the best of his knowledge, Amos Clebe had ignored his existence whenever their paths had happened to cross. The Judge had plainly considered himself in a walk of life far above that of the tall, black-haired cowboy who was tabbed as an Indian.

Now looking back at these things in the light of the moment when he had prevented Amos Clebe from committing murder, he wondered if the Judge hadn't been far more aware of him than he had pretended.

None of these questions had an answer. And, as the days passed, they seemed to grow more and more remote. In contrast to the past period of danger and tension, the three of them settled into an existence that was almost Elysian.

Food was no problem, at least for the time being. Their horses grew sleek on rich forage. The heat of summer lay over the basin, but there was always the stream and the lake in which to swim for the sake of coolness. They built shelters under the overhang of boulders for protection from the drenching thunderstorms that occasionally raged across the land.

Kinky Bob, perhaps for the first time in his life, felt really free. His mood changed. Light broke through the somber way of his life. In the evenings he would sing as he helped with the camp work. Songs that Lee nor Clemmy had ever heard. Songs of the mighty Mississippi River. Of the plantations. Songs that were praise of creation and the Creator. His voice was deep and melodious.

Clemmy quickly learned the words and joined in the spirituals. Lee listened. He knew now why the legend of Rose O'Neil was kept alive around the wagon fires. The magic of Rose O'Neil had not been lost when she had died.

Kinky Bob confirmed that. "You make ol' Kink want to cry when you sing like dat, Missy," he told Clemmy. "It's like de Golden Nightingale was here with us ag'in."

"You mean you heard my mother sing?" Clemmy exclaimed.

"Suah did, Missy. Many times. Never tired o' listenin' to de voice o' Rose O'Neil. I worked as handy man in a playhouse in San'tone, way back in Texas, where yore mother was singin'. I follered her to El Paso an' got a job swampin' in a music hall where she was appearin'. I heerd her sing in Denver City, too. She knowed me by name. She used to smile at me."

He was silent for a moment. "An' I saw her lay dead on de stage in Punchbowl," he added. "I wished I hadn't."

"What was she like?" Clemmy asked slowly. "What was she *really* like?"

Kink sought for words. He gazed around at the basin. It was sundown. Broken thunderheads were like golden ships in the sky, propelled by massive sails. They cast great, drifting shadows on the lake and on the flats of grass that rippled in the warming wind.

"She was like all dis," he said. "Beautiful! Happy! Alive! She liked everybody. Why, she even smiled at me. Treated me like I was a person."

Clemmy didn't ask any more questions. She busied herself with preparing the meal. But Lee saw that she was brushing away tears. Tears of happiness. And of sadness for a mother who was only a sweet memory from childhood.

Another week went by. During daylight hours, Lee and Kink, spelling each other, kept watch over the surrounding plains from a lookout point in the hills to the west which commanded the route by which they had entered the basin. No sign of pursuers appeared.

At times Clemmy took over the monotonous task. The lookout point was on a ridge nearly half an hour's ride from their camp along the stream. It commanded a full view of the basin as well as the sea of plains to the west and north.

Lee, arriving at the ridge to relieve Clemmy of the duty one afternoon, found her sitting cross-legged, her hands clasped back of her head, gazing at the basin. She was so absorbed, she did not seem aware of his arrival. She emerged from her thoughts with a start when he spoke.

"Daydreaming?" he asked.

She smiled. "Something like that."

"Wishing?"

She laughed again, self-consciously. "I'm afraid so."

"For what?"

"What does anyone wish for when they're daydreaming?"

He sat down beside her. "When I came to this basin two years ago I stood right on this spot for a long time, wishing for a lot of things. I pictured myself building a ranch house down there where we're camped. Of owning my own brand."

He paused for a long time while she sat silent, waiting. "I wished for other things," he finally said. "For everything a man wants in his house."

Neither of them spoke for a long time. Neither of them dared. For they knew what was in their hearts.

"Why didn't you apply for—?" she finally began.

She broke off the question, seeing the expression in his face.

"Indians can't take up land," he said. "In Texas or in New Mexico either. We're in Texas now. You know that."

"But I told you—!" she began angrily.

"I know. But that doesn't mean it's that way."

He added grimly, "Kink believes I'm Comanch'. He's sure of it, in fact."

"He can be wrong. If he's so sure, why doesn't he say exactly why he is?"

"I'm afraid to ask," Lee said.

She arose. "There's no need to ask. And what difference would it make either way?"

Lee walked with her to her horse, saddled it, and gave her a hand when she mounted.

"You told me once that you had a wish come true," he said. "Was it worth wishing for?"

Again he saw color rise in her throat. "Yes," she said. Then she rode away.

He watched her emerge from the hills and head across the flat toward the camp. She looked back, and raised a hand, as though sure he was watching, as though she knew how much he had wanted to take her in his arms and tell her that she was all that mattered in life. But, because he loved her, he could never say these things to her.

They had seen no sign of the white stallion since their

return to the basin until the day Clemmy, coming in from lookout, reported sighting the horse and its band of mares.

"I spotted them north of the basin, out in the plains," she said. "They were foraging, but I'm sure they had come out of the basin. They must have been in for water last night."

"Around daybreak, most likely," Lee said. "That's the time the real wild ones usually come to water, especially a horse t' at's gone mustang after knowing what it's like to be in a corral. Those kind are the hardest to trap."

Kinky Bob's head lifted. "Trap?"

"If that's really Mike Bastrop's Barb stud, it's worth a try," Lee said.

"Ain't much chance it's de Barb," Kink argued. "Jest another broomie, most likely. Dar's white broomtails, jest like any other color. Not many, o' course. Anyway, what you aim to do, even if you ketched dat horse an' he turned out to be de Barb?"

"In addition to being a horse nobody could run down if one of us needed a real ride in a hurry, it's worth money," Lee said. "A lot of money." He eyed Clemmy.

"We can't live like this forever," he added. "And they won't keep on looking for us forever, either. It's my guess that they figure by this time that we've either gone under on the plains or have managed to get out of the country. And that's exactly what we'll have to do. We'll have a better chance now."

"To get out of the country?" Clammy asked.

"Yes. We've got to try for Mexico. Maybe we can swing back in a year or two. Maybe into California. Or into the upper Missouri River country. They say people don't ask too many questions in either of those places."

Clemmy gazed at him. "If we weren't with you, would you try to hide in Mexico?"

"What else?" Lee demanded.

"I'll tell you what else. You'd stay here as an outlaw until they ran you down. That's what you'd do. You'd die before you'd let them run you out of this range. You believe this is your home. That you belong here. You're talking of going to Mexico only because you think Kink and I would be better off there. That's the truth, isn't it?"

"Why wouldn't I be thinking about my own neck?" Lee snorted. "After all, they want to hang me for a murder I didn't do."

She wrinkled her nose at him. "Maybe. But you also know they might try to put Uncle Tice's killing onto me. In fact, it wasn't very long ago that you acted like you believed that yourself. For all I know, you still do."

"That's for you to worry about," Lee said, grinning. "But I believe we were talking about trying to get a rope on that white stallion, instead of around our own necks. A trader would pay a thousand or more for that horse on sight, if it really is the Barb. Some of those rich *hacendados* down around Chihuahua might pay a heap more for him, and no questions asked."

"So you want to add another horse-stealing to your record?" she said.

"They can only hang me once," Lee answered. "If that's Mike Bastrop's Barb, it now ought to belong to anyone who can catch it. It's been running wild for three years. If that's stealing, so be it."

Kink uttered an uneasy guffaw of derision. "Yo're ridin' a horse you ain't caught yit, Jack-Lee. If dat's de Barb, he's a ghost horse, I tell you. If'n you git a rope on him, he'll turn into a skilligan with a hoodoo ridin' him."

"That's a chance we'll have to take," Lee said.

"Worse'n dat, if he ain't a ghost, he'll suah be a killer, Jack-Lee. I don't want no more part o' dat stallion. The Majah blamed me for lettin' him git away. Dat Barb busted two o' my ribs when I tried to ride him. Left me layin' in de corral, an' jumped an eight-pole fence. Jest disappeared into de sky. You remember dat, Jack-Lee."

"I heard about it," Lee said. "I was up the trail with a drive when it happened. How old would that Barb be?"

Kink counted on his fingers. "He were only a three-year-old when he was shipped acrost de ocean. He'll be goin' on seven, I reckon."

"Right in the prime," Lee said. "I've got a hunch that white speck we've sighted is the same horse. What was it he was called?"

"El Rey somethin' or other," Kirk said. "Nobody could make out the rest o' the name them foreigners had registered. Majah Bastrop said pure-white Barbs are mighty scarce an' was rode only by kings an' nabobs in de old days. Ordinary folks was put to death for even tryin' to own one."

"We've got to stake out before daybreak down the basin until we can get a good look at that stud," Lee said. "The chances are that we're riding a blind trail and that horse will turn out to be a broomtail after all. The Barb's likely been dead for years."

It was still pitch dark the next morning when Lee and Kinky Bob crawled to a rise of ground that would give them a closer view of the meadows south of the lake where the wild horses grazed after coming in for water.

What breeze was drawing was light and intermittent, and in their favor. "Let's hope it won't shift," Lee murmured. "One scent of us and we'd never again get close enough to have a chance, if that's really the Barb."

They lay motionless and silent. Dawn was faint in the sky when they heard the wild ones coming. The horses were more than a quarter of a mile away, mere shadows in the dim light as they drank in the shallows, then scattered to graze in the marshy flats.

They finally could make out the ghostly figure of the white stallion. The animal stood motionless at a distance, head poised, legs braced. It was standing guard while the mares in its *manada* drank and grazed.

But, was it the Barb?

Presently it moved to water and drank deeply. It threw up its head suddenly and stood like a statue, muzzle keening the air. It had caught some hint of danger.

Daylight had strengthened so that the true magnificence of the animal was apparent. It was the Barb!

Lee glanced at Kink, and saw confirmation in the big man's face. And superstitious dread also.

The stallion left the margin of the lake. Its call came loud and imperious. The mares obeyed. The band wheeled like a cavalry troop, and then was off and away, heading out of the basin, eastward toward low hills beyond which lay the rolling plains.

"Dat debbil horse, he knew we was here," Kinky Bob whispered.

"Maybe," Lee said. "Maybe not. I've got a feeling it was something else that spooked him."

He watched the receding band of mares. He could not

make out the white Barb among them. Suddenly, he pointed and said, "There's your answer. Loafers. The Barb picked up their scent, not ours."

Two gray wolves were moving in the wake of the retreating *manada*. Big, savage plains wolves.

As they watched, doom suddenly materialized in the path of the loafers. The white stallion had leaped from hiding. The wolves tried to whirl and escape. But it was too late for one. It was trampled to death by the hoofs of an animal that had turned into a screaming, savage-eyed demon. The second wolf, which was the female, managed to flee into the brush.

Kinky Bob drew a long breath as they watched the stallion continue to vent its fury on the carcass of the wolf. The wind brought the wild, eerie bugling.

"Like I said," Kink whispered. "Dat's not a horse, dat's a debbil."

"But he'll come back to the basin," Lee said. He had never seen an animal as magnificent, as free, as self-sufficient.

They returned to camp. "He's a horse fit for kings to ride, sure enough," he told Clemmy.

"Or for a war chief to own and brag about," she said.

"War chief?"

"Such as a Comanche chief," she said. "Such as Eagle—"

Kinky Bob, who had been busy at the cookfire, straightened. "No!" he boomed. "No, Missy. Don't you never—"

"Such as Eagle-in-the-Sky," she continued.

There was a space of silence. "Eagle can tell you the truth about what you are and where you came from, Lee Jackson," she went on. "The only one who can. He says he is your father. But he never treated you like a son. He's a chief. He won't talk unless it's worth while. He might—"

"Don't listen to her," Kinky Bob implored. "Let sleepin' dogs lie still, Jack-Lee. Let's all take ourselves into Mexico an' be safe."

"Eagle might talk if you dangled something in front of him that he really wanted," Clemmy went on relentlessly.

She added, "Such as the Barb."

"Don't do it," Kink wailed. "You saw what dat debbil horse did to de wolf. He kill you too, Jack-Lee, if'n you try to ketch him."

Lee stood gazing almost unseeingly at Clemmy. She

watched him for a time, then said, "It's got to be faced. It's got to be settled."

"You know what it might mean, don't you?" he asked.

She was suddenly ashen. "Yes. It doesn't have to be that way. But it will be. I know you too well to expect anything else."

What she meant was that she was aware that if he learned that he really was the son of the Comanche chief, she would never see him again.

"I can't go on this way," she said. "You know how it is with me."

Lee turned to Kinky Bob. "You're not as afraid of that Barb as you try to make out," he said. "But you don't want me to talk to Eagle, do you, Kink?"

"What good would it do, Jack-Lee?"

"It would settle many things. You've refused to tell me why you are so sure I'm Comanche by birth. Why are you so certain, Kink?"

"I tell you I don't want to talk about it, Jack-Lee."

"You're going to tell me. Now!"

Kinky Bob was cornered. He said grimly, "You are Comanch', Jack-Lee. Nothin' kin ever change dat. Don't ever try. 'Taint no use."

"How do you know this? Why are you so sure?"

"One o' dem Comancheros tell me."

"Comanchero?"

This was a term for men who traded mainly with the tribes, but sometimes with settlers. Although it was a fading occupation, now that the Indians had taken reservation, there were still a few of these nomads around. The majority of them were of mixed blood, usually of Mexican-Indian extraction. They were trusted by the tribes and had often been the only link of communication between the settlers and the hostile Comanche Nation.

Kinky Bob nodded. "This one come by Rancho Verde years ago when you was still a young sprout. He stayed with Kinky Bob a few nights to rest his mules. He seen you. He told me de Army tried to run a high blaze on de Majah an' that he knew you was an Injun."

"He was sure of that?"

Kink nodded. "He'd lived in Chief Eagle's village. Seen you dar as a child. He even knew your Indian name."

"My Indian name? Even I never heard that. It was taboo in the village."

"De Comanchero say your name was Wa-no-lo-pay," Kink said.

Lee's lips were taut, colorless. Despair was in his eyes. "Wa-no-lo-pay?" he repeated. "That settles it."

Clemmy spoke. "You mean you had heard that name?"

Lee nodded. "Once, when I was a child, after I had been brought to Rancho Verde that name popped into my mind from somewhere. From a long way back. I don't know where. I suppose I'd heard it before the taboo was ordered in the village."

Memories crowded him, harsh and unwanted. "I uttered that name. Wa-no-lo-pay. Mike Bastrop went wild. He beat me with his belt. He told me it was a bad word and I was never to mention it again."

He looked at Clemmy, and there was utter desolation in his eyes. "I'm sorry," he said.

"And I'm glad," she replied. "Glad for you and for myself, John Lopez Calvin."

Lee stood gazing at her. She repeated it. "John Lopez Calvin. That was the full name of the little boy they took away with them when they raided Rancho Verde."

She added softly, "Juano Lopey. John Calvin's widow was Spanish, remember. She was a Lopez. Don't you understand? John Lopez Calvin. Juan Lopez Calvin. Wano Lopey. That's the Spanish way of giving a pet name to a child. You weren't much more than a baby when the Comanches stole you, but you could repeat your name. The only name you knew. The one your mother used. Juano Lopey."

Lee rolled a cigaret with shaking fingers, spilling some of the treasured dry makings from his dwindling supply. Clemmy lifted a burning twig from the fire and held it to the quirly, and she and Kinky Bob stood waiting for him to speak.

He pulled smoke deep into his lungs. "One of you is right," he finally said. "You, Clemmy—or the Comanchero."

He looked around. "First, we've got to catch the Barb," he said.

Kinky Bob spoke, almost hopefully. "Maybe he won't

never come back here." The big man plainly believ
Clemmy was giving Lee a path that would only lead
disappointment. "Maybe he already know we after hi
Maybe he lay fer us like he did for de wolves."

"How would he know we're after him?" Clemmy
manded.

"If I could answer that, Missy, I'd be able to vanish i
flash of fire. Dar are things that know everything. Sc
has the shape o' humans, some look like animals. But t
ain't neither human nor animal."

"I don't believe you take any stock in such thi
yourself," Clemmy said. "You're just trying to stop
from talking to that Comanche chief."

However, the Barb and his *manada* did not return
next day. Nor the next, nor the next. Lee and Kinky I
lay on watch as each day dawned. Except for the scr
ny, long-tailed mustangs that came in, the marshes
mained deserted.

There had been evidence of thunderstorms out on
plains. That could mean that the stallion and his m
had no need to come into the basin for water.

Hot, dry weather set in. Searing weather.

CHAPTER ELEVEN

It was the fifth morning of their vigil. Dawn was a promise in the sky when Lee came suddenly to attention. Kinky Bob sighed. Clemmy, who had come out with them in the darkness, tired of being alone in camp, drew a deep breath.

The wild ones had returned to the basin. And the big Barb was there with his *manada*.

"All right," Lee said, after the horses had headed back to the plains. "This is going to take time. Weeks, maybe. One mistake and he'll be gone forever out of reach."

The Barb came back the next morning, and the next. Lee mapped out the route the stallion used in coming in from the open plains. Through one area in the hills, the Barb and his mares followed a dry wash for more than half a mile. The wash was wide and flat for the most part, but narrowed at one point for a distance of nearly two hundred yards between cut banks eight to ten feet high.

"There's our only chance," Lee said. "And that's the Barb's mistake. He's used that path so many times he's sure he's safe and has grown careless."

There were ample deadfalls of willow and ash and cottonwood and wild pecan available in the basin. The three of them, with the help of the horses, spent their days moving poles, roughly ax-cut to ten-foot lengths, into position on the flats above the bottleneck in the wash.

Lee and Kinky Bob killed deer, doing their hunting far up the basin and only when they were sure the wild ones were out on the plains.

From the hides, the three of them laboriously cut strips, which they braided into rawhide thongs. Using the thongs, they laced the poles together into crude sections that could be handled by two persons, and lashed to form barricades. The green hide shrank as it dried in the hot days, clamping the poles rigidly.

Every move was made with extreme caution. The major

part of the task was performed in the blazing heat
midday when the quarry was least likely to return. Th
were periods when the Barb and his mares failed
appear in the basin for days at a time. When this occur
they were beset by the fear the stallion had beco
suspicious and their labor had gone for nothing. E
always, the wild band would show up again, following
same route along the wash.

"We gittin' mighty low on flour, salt, an' a lot o' otl
things," Kinky Bob said one morning. "Looks like K
better take a *paseo* fer a few days to see what he l
round up."

"Where would you do this rounding up?" Lee asked.

"Might hit a line camp or two in de Armadillos," K
explained. "All de outfits will be stockin' de camps w
grub this time o' year to git ready fer winter. Cain't cle
out a camp, o' course. Jest take a dab here an' a ċ
there. Don't want to make 'em suspect we're still arou
I'll finish up with whatever else we need from Jue
Clebe's pantry."

"Judge Clebe's pantry?"

"He got plenty o' supplies an' he'll never miss w
Kink takes. Celia say he never even check up on what s
buys."

"I thought so. All this urge to fatten up our larder
only an excuse to ride into town to see your lady frier
You fool, if you're caught they'll string you up."

"Ain't goin' to be caught, Jack-Lee. An' if you're w
ryin' about Celia, I kin tell you dat she won't never t
nothin' to nobody."

Kink added, "An' she kin tell us what's goin' on. She
know whether they're still lookin' fer us, or whetl
they've give up."

It was this argument that swayed Lee. They were d
perately in need of news. "I'll give you four days,"
said. "If you're not back by then, I'll come looking i
you."

"Don't never do dat, Jack-Lee," Kink said grimly. "I
ain't back in dat time, it'll be 'cause dey got me. An' ċ
will figure you'll come in, lookin' fer me. Dey'll be wait
for you."

Kinky Bob returned only a few hours ahead of the fc

day limit that Lee had set. He was saddle-worn, but grinning. He had a bulging bag of supplies on his horse.

"De Majah's give up any idea o' startin' a late beef drive up de trail dis year," he reported. "He seems to have too many other things to keep him busy. You ain't de only one what's got a price on yore head, Jack-Lee. I ain't one to brag, but de Majah is offerin' a thousand dollahs in gold to anyone what fetches in ol' Kink, dead or alive. Now who'd ever have figgered I'd be worth that much on de hoof?"

"We've been worrying ourselves sleepless, waiting for you to show up, and you come back swelled up because you've got a bounty on your scalp," Lee commented. "What about Judge Clebe? Is he still in El Paso?"

"No. He back in Punchbowl, presidin' over court, which is back in session. But he brung back three tough gentlemen with him from El Paso. Bodyguards. Celia says she's gittin' mighty tired o' them bein' always around de house an' havin' to be fed an' took care of."

"Bodyguards? For the Judge?"

"Gun quicks. Bad men, dey is, Celia say. Dey go wherever de Judge goes. De Judge says his life has been threatened by some pals o' a bunch o' rustlers dat he sent to prison about a year ago."

Lee and Clemmy looked at each other. "Maybe Mike Bastrop knows it was the Judge and not me who put that slug in him," Lee said.

"I'm sure of it," Clemmy said.

"You mean dem two are gunnin' fer each other?" Kink demanded disbelievingly. "De Majah an' de Judge? Why would dey do dat?"

Lee shrugged. "I wish I knew." There could only be conjectures. Only one thing seemed certain. Whatever the cause, it went back to the night Bill Tice had been killed. The easiest answer was that the feud had been touched off by a quarrel over their poker game.

But Clemmy had said big money was never involved in the games, contrary to popular belief. Perhaps the stakes were higher than she believed. At least, Amos Clebe was certain to have some sort of income aside from the modest salary the county paid its presiding judge. It was assumed that he had investments, which, along with his

poker winnings, permitted his way of living—a luxurio[u]
furnished mansion, diamonds, fine cigars and whisky,
elaborate entertainment of flashy ladies on his trips ou[t]
town to El Paso and San Antonio and Denver.

"What about the Tice brothers?" Clemmy asked Ki[nk]
Bob.

"Celia said dem scamps spend de most o' their tim[e]
town now, drinkin' an' gamblin'. Dey got plenty o' mo[ney]
now dat dey've inherited BT. Dey've gone an' hired th[em]
selves some gunpackers too, dat hang around with dem [all]
de time."

"More bodyguards?" Lee exclaimed. "The Judge,
now the Tices! It looks like a lot of people we know [are]
out to punch the tickets of somebody. With bullets."

"Are Merl and Gabe still looking for us?" Clem[my]
asked. "Personally, I mean."

"Maybe not personally, Missy, but Celia say someb[ody]
is seein' to it dat notices o' Mike Bastrop's reward offe[r]
bein' posted all over Texas an' New Mexico. She say [she]
heard dat de word has gone down even into Mexico [dat]
de Majah will pay anybody who fetches you back ac[ross]
de river, Jack-Lee."

"Strapped dead to a pack mule, of course," Lee said.

"I reckon dat's de truth of it," Kink said gloomily. "[De]
man still want you dead, an' he ain't goin' to give up [till]
you is. Looks like we'll have to find someplace else t[o go]
an' hide."

"You think they'll find this place?" Lee asked.

"Five thousand dollahs keeps men thinkin', Jack-Le[e. I]
don't reckon we kin keep on robbin' line camps, or dep[end]
in' on Celia to supply us from de Judge's kitchen wit[hout]
somebody gittin' on our trail."

"You're right, of course," Lee said. "I've got a fee[ling]
we've about run out our string here. Sooner or l[ater]
somebody will remember stories about a Spirit Lake [out]
here, and really begin to look for it."

"We got to go a long, long way to git away from [de]
Majah," Kinky Bob said. "He is a stubborn man. W[hat's]
dis place I hear men talk about at times? Dis Argen[tine]
place. Lots o' outlaws go dar when things git too hot [for]
dem around here. Is it in de United States?"

"No," Lee said. "But maybe we better go there. It's

enough away so that even Mike Bastrop isn't likely to ever have us brought back."

He added, "But we'll need money to travel that far. We're about all set to try for the Barb. We'll make sure we know exactly what to do, and then make our move when the sign is right."

The sign seemed right three days later. The three of them crouched close to earth, listening as the wild ones streamed down the wash toward the basin.

Lee kept restraining hands on both Clemmy and Kinky Bob, forcing them to wait, for they were as taut as drawn bowstrings. The thud of hoofs came abreast, then moved steadily on down the defile toward the basin.

Dawn lighted the ridges. A cold wind rattled the brush. The drumbeat of the hoofs of a single horse sounded in the wake of that of the main band. Lee chanced a quick glimpse and sank back. He waited until all sounds had faded into the distance.

"All right," he said. "That was the Barb, following his *manada* in. Let's go!"

They burst into activity. He and Kinky Bob, working at a run, carried, one by one, the sections of the barrier they had made and hidden beyond the rim of the coulee. They set the sections, bracing them with poles, and Clemmy lashed them together to form a barricade across the outer end of the bottleneck.

They were spent and soaked with cold sweat when Lee was satisfied that that part of the trap was as secure as possible. They hurried to the inner end of the bottleneck and crouched in hiding in brush above the rim.

Other sections of the second barricade lay close at hand. These were of lighter poles because there would be little leeway in time when they must be set in place. A stumble, a few seconds' delay, and their plan would fail.

They lay waiting, listening. Their laboring lungs quieted. Daylight strengthened. They did not speak, for Lee had warned them against conversation. He had seen samples of the acuteness of hearing of wild horses. The Barb, once having been dominated by man, would be quick to identify such an alien sound and would be gone with the wind.

The wait went on and on. Lee, watching the first rays

of sunshine glint on the rims of the Armadillos, began to fear that the wild ones were not following their normal routine. Then they heard the wild ones returning. The sound of hoofs came nearer. Lee fought back the urge to rise to his knees and take a look. That might have been fatal.

The Barb should be bringing up the rear, as usual. His habit was to remain well back of his harem, both to avoid dust and to punish any straggler.

The roll of hoofs came abreast in the coulee and receded eastward. A few seconds later they heard the lone horse pass by.

"Now!" Lee breathed.

They had rehearsed it several times at a distant spot and using imaginary items.

They arose, carrying the sections of the rawhide-bound barrier, slid over the lip of the cut bank into the wash, and frantically began bracing the sections in place to block the route of escape.

Up the wash, a bedlam arose. Mares were milling and screaming in confusion. They had found their path blocked by the upper barricade.

"Hurry!" Lee panted, jamming more poles in place to brace the new line.

A demon appeared in the draw. The Barb! The stallion had whirled to return, hoping to escape by the way he had entered the trap. He screamed in almost humanlike fury when he saw that his retreat was blocked by another of the terrible contrivances that had panicked the mares.

He came at the barrier, rearing, striking the poles with savage hoofs. Lee saw white teeth bared, grinding at the poles.

The mares also came thundering back, seeking escape. This was the moment Lee had foreseen as decisive for success or failure. For victory and freedom for the Barb, or capture and submission.

"Get out of here!" he shouted at Clemmy as he continued to push more poles in order to brace the barrier. "If they knock down that fence, you'll be trampled to jelly."

For once, she obeyed, scrambling to the lip of the cut bank to safety. "You too, Kink!" Lee gritted. "Get in the clear!"

The big man did not answer, but continued jamming

braces in place. A moment later a mass of frenzied wild horses came against the barrier.

The demoralized mares in the forefront reared back at the sight of the barricade, recoiling on the other animals. That saved the crude stockade, for Lee knew that it would never have stood against the full weight of the stampede. He knew that it also had likely saved his life and that of Kinky Bob's.

Once halted, the animals were victims of their own panic and indecision. The Barb was imprisoned among his own *manada*. He was rearing and bugling, but was almost helpless, jammed in among the mass of mares that stifled his efforts.

Lee and Kinky Bob scaled to opposite rims of the coulee and seized up the throw ropes they had placed there. The Barb screamed again—mournfully, despairingly. He remembered ropes! He remembered men!

As Lee spread the loop there was a sudden sickness in him. Up to this moment the Barb had been only an objective—a means to serve his purpose. A quarry to be outwitted and taken.

Face-to-face with this splendid creature, he was stung by guilt and self-reproach. It was as though the stallion was pleading for death rather than capture. This, he could understand. He, too, was a wild one who had fled to the plains to escape the confinement the Barb feared.

Clemmy was at his side. She sensed his hesitation, and its reason. "Please!" she screamed. "Throw!"

Lee flipped the loop over the rim of the cut bank and it settled precisely. Kinky Bob's rope joined it. Between them they had the Barb their captive.

The mares recoiled from their master who fought the ropes with appalling ferocity. They milled against the barrier, and it went down, opening a way to freedom. The *manada* fled down the draw and scattered on the open flat, heading for the plains.

But the Barb did not follow his mares. He was a prisoner. Lee and Kinky Bob finally brought the stallion to earth and hobbled him. He lay there for a long time. El Rey, the king, was no longer free.

"He goin' to die," Kinky Bob muttered and fingered the hoot-owl charm. "He'll come back to ha'nt us."

Lee stood looking down at their captive. The sickness

and the self-reproach increased. He and Kinky Bob and the horse were matted with sweat and dust.

The Barb did not die, whatever its own hope might have been. At last it drew a long, heaving breath that was almost a moan and struggled to its feet. It was prepared to fight to escape, but was forced to stand, trembling and helpless. The hobbles on its legs were the emblems of its despair.

Suddenly, Lee moved in, a knife in his hand. The stallion tried exhaustedly to strike at him, but failed. The blade slashed a hobble. Before he could continue, Clemmy rushed in, wrapping her arms around him, forcing him with her young strength away from the horse.

"No!" She had the same fierce spirit in this moment as the stallion, the same primitive determination.

"I can't do this," Lee said. "Alive or dead, that horse would haunt me the rest of my life. He doesn't deserve this. He won his freedom. He's been so alive, so free. It isn't worth it."

She continued to cling to him, pinning down his arms. "I know how you feel," she sobbed. "But you've got to do this. *We've* got to do this. Both of us. For your sake. For my sake. You can't be an outlaw all your life. They'll catch you sooner or later, just like the Barb was caught. I've felt from the moment we sighted this horse, that this was the right thing to do. The only thing. Maybe it sounds crazy, but it's as though this is an answer to a prayer. To my wish. As though this horse was here because you needed him. And because I needed him."

She added, her eyes warm and tender, "I have wished this. Night and day. Oh, how I've wished it."

She kissed him. She drew her head back and looked up at him. "You've got to try to make Eagle tell what you really are," she said. "For that's the only hope of having my wish come true. I love you, whatever you are or will be. I believe you love me, but I know that until you are sure what you are, I will always be lonely. It would make no difference to me what you are, but you'd always let it keep us apart. Destroy us both."

She continued to cling to him. He held her tight against him for a space, then his arms fell away. She had told the truth. He had seen what had happened to white women who had married Indians. He could not bring this on

Clementina O'Neil, daughter of Rose O'Neil. Clemmy, the loyal, the gentle, the one who would remain steadfast through all hardship, through all eternity.

"There may come a time," he said hoarsely, "when we will never see each other again. I want you to always remember that you will be the only one—the only love in my life."

She began to smile. She held a happiness that was pure and joyous. "I'll begin wishing once more," she said.

"For what?"

"The same thing for which I've been wishing ever since we came to this place. That some day this is where we will live and be happy. And free."

She added, "And that the Barb will come back here with us. I can wish that. I've told you that some of my wishes come true. Like the one in Punchbowl that day."

"In Punchbowl?"

"When you kissed me. I was wishing you'd do exactly that."

"You *are* a vixen, aren't you?"

"If that's what I have to be to get my wish, yes."

CHAPTER TWELVE

"Behold!" Clemmy said dramatically. "Admire the handi-work of the two best bronc peelers in New Mexico, and maybe all points east and west, not to mention north and south."

More then a week had passed since the capture of the Barb. The stallion stood, hipshot, on the fringe of camp, held by a hackamore and a picket rope, in addition to a hobble. He seemed to know he was the object of Clemmy's remark, for he came to attention, arched his neck, and cavorted.

"He's a showboat," Lee said. "Stands around admiring his own shadow. A real biscuit eater. That reminds me, and listen to what I say, girl! Quit feeding him biscuits. Let him rustle his own grub. You're spoiling a great horse by spoonfeeding. I don't want any fat on him. We may have riding to do."

"Who'd have thought he could have been gentled so soon?" she said.

"There's no such thing as gentling him. He's smart enough to act contented and ride the grub line—as long as there's a rope around his neck. All he's really waiting for is a chance to go back to his mares. Back to the plains."

He added, "And that's where he belongs."

Clemmy said nothing. It was sundown of a late August day. They were breaking camp.

They pulled out as dusk came. Clemmy rode her horse astride. Kinky Bob hazed the loaded packhorse ahead of them. Lee led the Barb. The stallion pranced along, skittish as a colt, plainly pleased to be on the move.

Lee and Kinky Bob had brought to bear everything they knew about the art of taming a horse, and had succeeded far more quickly than they had anticipated. Too quickly, Lee sometimes warned himself. The Barb, after a day or two of refusal, had abruptly decided to bow to the inevitable, and had accepted discipline without more than the expected protest. He had not objected to a bit and saddle, and had fought only mechanically when he was first mounted by Lee.

"Speed!" Lee had said in awe. "And strength. What a horse! I've never sat anything like this one."

"An' never will ag'in if'n you git careless," Kink had warned. "He's only waitin'. Don't let him fool you by actin' like he's given in. Remember, he was a tame horse at first. He knows humans, an' how to git along with 'em. An' how to wait for de right minute to go bad ag'in."

They headed northward, along the lonely stretches of the Llano Estacado. The thunderstorms of August were sweeping the plains regularly, and the natural basins and water tanks were full.

Their destination was the Comanche reservation on the Clear Fork of the Brazos River in Texas. The direction was generally northeastward over a country where there were few trails and where they saw occasional sign of the buffalo that were a vanishing breed. Lee said it would be more than a week's travel by the circuitous route they would be forced to follow in order to avoid settlements and ranches.

The moon was coming full. They intended to travel at night by its light as long as was feasible. An August moon. The Comanche war moon. For all its beauty, this was the moon the settlers had feared in the past because it had brought the Spearmen off the plains.

"Ain't no hostiles come down to kill an' skulp folks fer quite a spell," Kinky Bob said, "but dat don't mean dey won't paint ag'in, an' jump de reservation. What chance would we have if'n we run into a war party?"

Kink had never ceased opposing this mission. "Better to head fer Mexico, like we first said, Jack-Lee," he had argued, "Now dat we're comin' out into de open, sooner or later somebody's sure to ketch sight o' us. Den we'll have reward hunters on our trail. Even if'n we make it to dis Comanche camp dat you talk about, what den? Dis chief, Eagle, likely is daid after all dese years."

"I heard only a couple of months ago that Eagle-in-the-Sky was still alive and still head man in his village," Lee had said.

"But how you know he'll tell you anythin', even if you

git to talk to him? How you know he won't turn you over to de law? Maybe even de Comanches know you is wanted."

Lee had no answer. The same misgivings were heavy in his mind. The risk was great, and there was only a gambling chance that Eagle would divulge anything helpful. In addition, Kink might be right about the chief being dead. Eagle was now a very old man who could have been taken since Lee's last news of him.

There might be a few other oldsters in the village whose memories went back to the raid on Rancho Verde, but Lee's knowledge of the Comanche character told him that his chances of getting information that could be relied on from anyone other than the chief were remote indeed.

Eagle was his only hope. The chief would speak for all the village. He was above average in intelligence. Although he could speak Spanish and English, he usually scorned those languages and took the position that only the Comanche tongue was worth using.

Lesser members of the tribe would, no doubt, disclaim any connection with the Rancho Verde raid. Indians who had admitted such things in the past had been hung by the Army, or sent to the big, stone-walled lodge at Fort Leavenworth, never to return.

However, in spite of the cruelties he had suffered at Eagle's hands, Lee remembered the chief's pride. Eagle had fought for his people and his hunting grounds. He had a warrior's vanity in regard to his feats. He would be too proud to fear retaliation. Therefore, he might talk about the Rancho Verde raid if the reward was high enough.

Lee never relaxed vigilance over the Barb. He and Kink took turns at night, standing watch for intruders, but mainly to make sure that the picket lines and hobbles that held the stallion were secure.

They forded branches of the Colorado River and reached the drainage of the Brazos. They were now east of the Staked Plains, but following the rough country that broke away from the plateau. This was Comanche country, their old hunting grounds. To Lee, he was riding through scenes of his childhood. Often, disturbingly, landmarks would impinge on his memory as though he had passed this way only yesterday.

He became more and more silent. Occasionally they

sighted buffalo. Small bands, or lone animals. Remnants of
the great herds which still held out in the cedar brakes
and brushy canyons. This land was still as it had been.
Except for a few maverick cattle—mossy old longhorns—
that had escaped from the ranches to the east, there was
little sign of white men. The settlements still clung to the
watercourses on the easier land to the east. The big
ranches had yet to invade this area.

They forded a small creek. This, Lee recalled, was
where he had been beaten by the squaw who said she was
his mother because he had dropped a bundle of firewood
as he had tried to wade the stream when it was in flood.

They crossed a divide and emerged onto a stretch of
open country that brought memories more vivid than any
other. And more bitter. This was where the buffalo hunting camp had been pitched when he had made his third
and final attempt to escape. The entire village had been
quartered here while the hunters slaughtered buffalo that
had been stampeded into a trap in a box draw.

Lee had been about six years old at the time, and
forced to do a squaw's work. He had helped scrape and
stretch hides and carry water and wood from dawn until
dark, day after day. He had cut and strung strips of fleece
and humpmeat for drying, with squaws poking him to
greater activity with sticks and the lashes of dog whips.

He remembered many things. He remembered seizing
up a long spear that some buffalo hunter had thrust in the
ground upon returning from the hunt, and bringing its flat
metal head down on the skull of Eagle's eldest wife.

He had fled from the camp into the early darkness,
leaving the stunned squaw lying on the ground. She was
Wau-Qua, who said she was his mother. He remembered
the pursuit. They had tried for two days to catch him.
They would have succeeded, except that he had encountered the Army patrol and had surrendered.

He was remembering the hardships of his existence with
the Comanches. But his very familiarity with this country
seemed to prove everything in his mind that he wanted to
disprove. This, surely, must have been the land of his
birth.

Clemmy watched his silence continue. She said nothing,
but the carefree happiness that had come to her during
the days at Spirit Lake was now faded. She became again

the sharp-tongued, scornful Clemmy O'Neil with a chip on her shoulder. Defensive of mind, suspicious of the motives of others.

She had reverted, as Lee had reverted. He was Comanche now in mood and grimness, in wariness and training. She was the defiant, spitfire daughter of a notorious woman.

They lived off the country. Game could be had for the shooting, but they used their rifles sparingly. Wild turkeys were so plentiful they could be taken with club in the evenings when they weighed down the limbs of the groves of post oaks.

They abandoned night travel because the country was so wild and rough it became a problem to pick a feasible route even in daylight.

They had been on the way nearly a week without having sighted anything except wildlife, but one morning, as they were following a stream that Lee believed would join with the Clear Ford of the Brazos, they emerged into a wide stretch of open prairie. And halted.

Three riders were moving into scattered timber across the clearing. They were far away, but they seemed to be hazing along a loaded packhorse and at least three other pack animals with empty saddles.

"Freeze!" Lee warned. "Maybe they won't spot us."

The trio kept heading westward and vanished into the timber.

"Good!" Kink said. "Dey didn't see us." He added, "You reckon dey was law men lookin' fer us?"

"Hardly," Lee said. "Not way up here. We're almost in the Panhandle. Hunters, is my guess. They're probably out to get some buffalo robes. And heads. Robes and stuffed buffalo heads are said to be bringing a good price back East these days. They're getting mighty scarce."

However, toward sundown the following day, he glimpsed a lone rider far behind them. The horseman vanished into the country and did not reappear.

"Maverick hunter, maybe," Lee said. "Trying to build himself up a brand with a running iron."

They had spotted a number of wild cattle during the day. They knew there were ranches on the Clear Fork to the east.

The horse the man had been riding was of a light dun color. Lee remembered, uneasily, that one of the three strangers they had sighted the previous day had been riding a horse of that distinctive hue.

He backtracked, leaving Kink and Clemmy to ride ahead at a slower gait. He picked up the trail of the lone rider, followed it until he felt sure the man had shown no interest in their own trail, then returned to where Kink and Clemmy waited.

"I doubt if he even saw our trail," he said. "He seemed to be interested only in heading west."

They camped that night on what Lee believed was the Clear Fork. That meant they probably were already on the Comanche reservation. They had proof of that at daybreak.

They were awakened by shrill shouts in the distance and the thunder of wings. They rolled out of their blankets and crept on foot through the thickets until they could peer into another of the clearings that characterized this country.

An immense flock of wild turkeys that had left the timber at dawn in order to forage in the clearing had been surprised by a half-dozen young, mounted Indians.

The Indians had cut the birds off from refuge in the timber and were hazing them into taking wing. Racing on their ponies beneath the demoralized fowls, they kept their quarry aloft until the turkeys, exhausted, fell to earth where they were easy victims of clubs.

"Comanches," Lee said.

Again the memories came in a flood. He had seen turkey kills as a boy. It had meant hours of helping the squaws feather and prepare the birds for the gorging that customarily followed.

They crouched in hiding until the hunting party had left, their ponies loaded with the kill.

"There'll be a village not far away," Lee said. "I'll follow these fellows and get information. These might even be from Eagle's village. They were young braves, and I didn't know any of them, of course. There are other villages on the reserve, and Comanches always keep on the move."

He trailed the hunting party alone. He had traveled only a few miles when the wind brought a scent that again took him back to bitter years. It was the tang of wood-smoke, of buckskin and old buffalo-hide lodges, of fresh-cut firewood and humanity—all mingling with the incense of blooming lupine and willows and bluebonnets and buck-thorn. A Comanche village.

He located the lodges and scouted them from a dis-tance. The village stood among scattered trees along a small stream. The turkey hunters had arrived. Squaws and children were swarming about, unloading the game. Lee watched for a long time. He did not see any of the children poked with sticks, nor switched as he had been under the same circumstances. These Indian children were happy. It had been that way in the other days. He had been the only one who had been tormented.

He singled out one gray-haired, but drill-straight Indian who stood apart from the activity. The chief.

He retreated and rejoined Clemmy and Kink. They could see the news in his attitude.

"It is Eagle's—!" Clemmy began. She had started it bravely, but was unable to finish it. There was now a great terror in her. A doubt that her own belief was right. In Lee was the same grisly fear.

He nodded. "I saw him. He's aged, of course, but I'd know him anywhere."

He repeated it. "Anywhere. In hell, I'd know him."

He turned to Kink. "Shine up the Barb while I shave and slick up. We've both got to be at our best. Take him to the stream and wash him down. Comb out his mane and tail with whatever you can find to use. I want him to look like the king he is."

"You ain't goin' in dar alone, are you?" Kink de-manded.

"That's the only way it can be done."

"What if they figger out dat you used to be—to be—" Kink began to flounder helplessly.

"—One of them? I'm banking on it that Eagle *will* know me."

"Won't he hold it against you?" Clemmy spoke. "What if—he sees to it that you never come back?"

"I'm taking the Barb in with me. Comanches don't kill a guest that brings gifts. That's against their code."

"He'll only take your gift and laugh at you," she said.

"It's also the Indian code that if a gift can't be returned with one of equal value, it must be refused. The Eagle has only one thing of value to me and he knows it."

"He'll lie to you."

"I doubt that. He's a chief. A Comanche chief. Whatever else he might be, he'd lose face if he lied. There's a matter of pride and dignity involved. Eagle will either have to tell me what I want, or he'll have to refuse to accept the Barb."

He looked at the stallion which Kink had washed down at the stream and was now currying, using a handful of dry grass as a comb. "I believe it will come mighty hard for Eagle to give up that horse, once he lays eyes on him. He will want a mount like that on the other side. That will make him a chief again."

"De other side?" Kink asked uneasily. "You ain't meanin' de happy land, now is you?"

"White men call it the Happy Hunting Ground," Lee said. "Indians have other names for it, the most of which are taboo for speaking. Only medicine men can say the words. It's the custom to be buried with a string of their best ponies when they go. They don't want to be afoot on the other side."

"You mean dey'd destroy dis fine animal when dat Injun died?"

"That's the custom."

Kink stopped furbishing the animal. He dropped the bundle of grass and walked off into the brush, muttering to himself. Clemmy refused to meet Lee's eyes. She also walked away.

Lee shaved, using a still pool of water as an unsatisfactory mirror. He put on his spare shirt which he had washed out when they had camped the previous night. He dusted his boots, saddled his roan, and led up the Barb.

Kink did not appear. However, Clemmy came hurrying to his side. "You will come back," she said huskily. "You *will*. I wish it."

"Of course," he said.

She placed a hand on the shoulder of the Barb. "Blame me for this," she sobbed. "Not yourself."

Lee rode away without looking back, leading the stallion. The sun was far down the afternoon sky.

As he appeared in sight of the Comanche village, the dogs, as usual, came charging to challenge a stranger. They came in a pack, with teeth gleaming and with shrill, coyotelike screaming. Also, as usual, they turned tail and ran howling when he charged his horse at them.

There were now less than a score of lodges in Quin-a-se-i-co's village. Once he had been chief over ten times that number. Now the lodges, made of buffalo leather, were old and patched. The colorful designs that had been painted on them were faded. The picture stories of the past mighty deeds of the warriors of the village had been dimmed by time and weather. Some of the Comanches even lived in shabby canvas Sibley tents that had been given them by the Army—a sacrifice of pride for these people who had been the great buffalo hunters of the plains—the Spear People, other tribes had called them.

Squaws were still busy preparing the turkeys the hunters had brought in. They and the naked children stared at the rider entering the village. It was the big, pale horse he was leading that fascinated them.

The squaws suddenly began scurrying to hiding, dragging children with them. Warriors appeared and stood motionless, waiting for the visitor to disclose his intentions.

The chief's lodge stood near the medicine pole in the center of the village. The lodge was made of buffalo hide in the ancient manner and bore the scars of time.

A squaw peered from its entrance. Lee remembered that woman, even though the years had withered her. She was Wau-Qua, who had said she was his mother. She was now as lean as a starving crow, and snag-toothed. How well he remembered Wau-Qua and her genius for inventing ways of tormenting him.

He gazed at hostile faces and into fierce, suspicious eyes. Somehow, this gave him hope. They did not see him as one of them. They saw him as an alien.

The Comanches had smoked the peace pipe with the Army, and had signed the treaties that restricted them to a segment of what had once been their vast domain. But, their pride had not been crushed.

There were faces that bore the scars of war. Some of these warriors, no doubt, had the scalps of white men and women hidden in their lodges—forbidden by the Army, but treasured and flaunted when coup dances were held and appeals offered that the ghosts of all departed fighters would return with spears in their hands to restore the race to its former place in the sun.

CHAPTER THIRTEEN

He held his horse to a walk as he rode through the village. The Barb seemed to sense that it was the object of attention, for it pranced along, its mane and tail flying.

Lee halted his mount in front of Eagle's lodge. The flap was closed. The interior was silent, but a faint haze of smoke from the cookfire drifted from the wings above. The feathered lance of a chief was driven in the ground alongside the entrance—the historic notification that Eagle was at home.

"I am one who lived in the lodge of Quin-a-se-i-co," he spoke loudly in English. Then he changed to the Comanche tongue. "I come to talk with him. I bring him a gift. A horse that only a chief must ride."

He rode closer to the lodge and looped the Barb's picket line around the lance.

He remained in the saddle, waiting. The village street was now deserted. Every Comanche had retreated into his lodge. This, too, was historic custom. A stranger had come to talk to the chief. He had brought a gift. A gift such as none of them had ever even dreamed of possessing. A gift that might bring fame to all of them because of its magnificence. For the Comanche was, above all, a horseman. A horse was his strength, his pride.

For a long time there was no response, as was befitting the dignity of a chief. Lee had known it would be this way. He knew all their ways—too well. Even the Comanche tongue, which he had seldom used since his escape from them as a boy, had come back easily—too easily.

The flap of the lodge was finally lifted. Eagle-in-the-Sky stepped into the open sunlight. The Comanche chief was still straight and tall, but gaunt. Time had frosted his brows and furrowed his cheeks. He wore a beaded vest, beaded elkhide breeches with belled bottoms in the Spanish style, and high, bleached moccasins. He had a beaded band around his whitening hair, and a small silver bell tinkled faintly as it hung from his pierced right earlobe.

His nose was hawklike. He bore many scars of battle, but there was one in particular that ran from jawbone into his hair, as jagged as a streak of lightning.

He gazed at Lee without speaking. Lee said, "I am Wa-no-lo-pay. You claimed I was your son."

Eagle continued to gaze, then said, "You are Wa-no-lo-pay. That is the truth. I know you after all these years."

His eyes turned to the pale horse. In spite of himself, he was unable to entirely maintain his pose of haughty indifference. Desire shone in his old eyes.

Then Eagle remembered the rules. The glint faded out of his eyes. Regret came. And anger. Anger at Lee for placing before him such a temptation.

Then he remembered that Lee would also know the Comanche code. Therefore he must feel that Eagle had something of equal value to the stallion and had come for it.

"We will smoke," Eagle said.

He motioned Lee to dismount, and led him into the lodge. Wau-Qua and a second squaw hovered in the background. At Eagle's order, the two women left the lodge. Wau-Qua cast a terrified glance over her shoulder as she hurried out. She feared that Lee had returned to square the account for the torments she had inflicted on him as a child.

Lee gave her a threatening scowl. He owed her that much, at least. She fled from the lodge in a panic. She probably feared that she was the gift he would ask in return for the white stallion.

Eagle lighted the pipe in the ancient ceremonial manner, sent smoke to the winds, and passed it over to Lee, who followed suit. The pipe passed back and forth three times, the ceremonial when a guest was being granted the favor of speaking to the chief.

"You have grown into a tall warrior, my son," Eagle finally said. "No one in the village can look over your head."

"I'm not your son," Lee said. "Not a real son, given to you by Wau-Qua or any of your wives. That is the truth, is it not, Quin-a-se-i-co?"

Eagle was a long time answering. He and Lee could hear the snuffling and impatient pawing of the Barb. Its shadow flickered against the wall of the lodge.

"You should be proud to be a chief's son," Eagle said.

"Am I Comanche?" Lee asked.

"You are as dark as a Comanche. You are as tall as a Comanche. Strong as a Comanche. You talk Comanche."

The chief was evading. It was the classic way of avoiding a falsehood.

"Am I Comanche?" Lee demanded again.

Eagle sat motionless on the robe. He thought it over for a long time, shooting speculative glances at Lee.

"You are not Comanche!" he finally said. "You are not my son."

Lee's heart thudded. He believed he was hearing the truth. However, there was the possibility that avarice had overcome Eagle's code of honor and that he was lying in hope he was offering a gift that would repay for the stallion.

"How can I know this?" Lee demanded.

"I tell you it is the truth," Eagle said haughtily.

"It is not enough," Lee said. "I must have proof."

"It is my gift to you," Eagle said. "That is what you came here to hear me say, is it not? I have said it."

He moved. He produced a rifle from beneath the robe. He cocked it and leveled it at Lee's heart. He suddenly spoke in English. "You are white man!" he uttered the words with hatred. "You are not Comanche."

Lee did not move. "It is no gift. Not until I have more than your word to show that you don't lie. If I am white, where did the Comanches find me?"

Eagle touched the long, jagged scar on his face. "This was given me by white woman," he said bitterly. "She is the one who bore you. She try to kill me. She do this to me."

"And *you* killed *her!*" Lee said hoarsely. "You killed my mother. The Comanches killed everyone at Rancho Verde that day except me. I was a small boy, not two years old. That's the truth, isn't it?"

Eagle did not speak. Lee waited. The seconds went by, marked by the throb of his pulse. He had come so near, and still was not sure.

"I will kill the horse unless I hear the truth," he said. His six-shooter was in his hand, looking back at Eagle over the rifle. "I will kill you, Eagle-in-the-Sky, if you shoot me now. I will live long enough to pull the trigger of this gun. You will die. The horse will not be yours. He will still be mine to ride beyond the far mountain. You know more about me than you have told. I want this knowledge. All of it."

Eagle sat motionless for a long time. Then he made a scornful gesture of acceptance. Laying aside the rifle, he arose, moved stiffly across the lodge, and drew a wolf pelt aside. Lee saw a chest the size of a small trunk. It was made of polished oak, brass-bound, the type in which valuables had been kept by ranchers in the early days. Its lock had been torn off long ago.

Eagle lifted its lid and delved into it. In the saffron light that filtered through the hide walls, Lee made out trinkets of many kinds—gold watches, bone and pearl buttons, combs, and brooches. Lace and silk kerchiefs, all soiled by time and coup-counting. Here was the record of a warrior's life. His coup chest!

There were items in the chest far more grim. Tufts of hair. Scalps. Some were those of Indians who had been tribal enemies, but the majority were from the heads of settlers. From men and women and children. These were souvenirs of raids on cabins, of ambushed stagecoaches, of men shot down in their cornfields.

One scalp was of fine, long, dark hair, faded by time, but retaining some of what must have once been young, lustrous beauty. Lee was suddenly gazing at Eagle through a haze of fury.

"My mother's hair?" he demanded.

The chief did not answer, but the truth was in his eyes.

"I know now why I've always hated you, Quin-a-se-i-co," Lee said, reverting to the Comanche tongue. "I thought it was a nightmare that I remembered from babyhood. But it was real, wasn't it? I *saw* you murder my mother. I was a child in her arms. That sight stayed with me."

Eagle had never been nearer death, not even when the bullet fired by Lee's mother had torn that jagged line up his face. He looked into the muzzle of Lee's six-shooter with the scorn of a warrior. He had faced this thing too many times in the days when life was dear to him to fear it now in his declining years.

"A great medicine man told me long ago that you

would be the cause of my death, Wa-no-lo-pay," he said. "He told me you would see me lying dead at your feet."

"So now you can utter my name," Lee said. "Wa-no-lo-pay. John Lopez Calvin. That was why you forbade the tribe to speak that name. You never wanted me to hear it for fear I would know you had murdered my mother."

The chief did not answer.

"So that is why you hated me," Lee went on. "You were afraid what the medicine man said would come true. You feared that if I learned you had murdered my mother, I would kill you. You wanted me to die. You did not dare kill me yourself, because you had claimed me as a son, and it is forbidden to shed one's own blood. You put the squaws on me to torment me, hoping I would die. But, when I ran away, you wanted me brought back, for fear I would come back some day to pay you for what you did."

Lee added, "I am here."

Eagle still did not speak. He turned to the coup chest and drew out a small, brass strongbox. It was the type in which documents and jewelry were kept for safekeeping.

Eagle offered the box. "I give this to you," he said.

Lee did not respond for a time. Refusal meant failure and that he must leave the village, taking the Barb with him. Acceptance might also mean failure. Eagle was offering him a gift in return for the horse. But the strongbox might be empty.

"You want?" Eagle demanded.

Lee said, "Yes. I want it."

Eagle placed the box in his hands. His heart sank. The metal made it heavy—but not heavy enough. There could be little or nothing inside.

The small key was still in the lock. It refused to turn at first, its brass corroded by time. Finally, it yielded. He lifted the lid on its small, squeaking hinges.

All that the box offered was a sheet of paper and a faded photograph. If it had contained any valuables, Eagle long ago had made away with them.

"You read?" Eagle asked.

Lee lifted the sheet of paper. It was the quality a well-to-do, refined woman would use for correspondence, and had therefore stood up under the rigors of time. It bore an embossed seal that was a reproduction of Rancho Verde's original Spanish cattle brand.

The upper half of the letter was unmarred, though soiled, but an ugly, dark blotch discolored the lower half of the sheet. The ink was faded. Lee threw open the flap of the lodge to admit more light. The major portion of the writing was still legible. It was written in the neat hand of a woman.

It was dated more than twenty years in the past. Lee read the words:

My Dearest Rose:

I have received your note, saying you are to be the bride of Clement O'Neil, and I am sending my wishes for a lifetime of happiness. I understand some busy-bodies are advising you against your choice, for Mr. O'Neil seems to be a man who enjoys life and lets no person tell him how he must live it.

I will tell you a secret. They said the same things when I married my beloved John Calvin. They said he was a gambler and a drifter who would only break my heart. He gave me only loyalty, joy, and devotion for the few years we had together. So to perdition with the pessimists. Life is short. I intend to dance at your wedding.

I have made my will, Rose dear, and have taken the liberty of naming you guardian of my little Juano in case anything should happen to me. You are the one person I am sure would love and look after him until he can fend for himself. I have made provision for you from the ranch income so that you will be compensated, of course.

Judge Clebe drew up the document for me. He and your former precious brother-in-law signed the paper as witnesses. Both have copies of the document, for safety's sake. I refer to William Tice, of course. I admit I would have preferred someone else as a witness to my will, but he happened to be handy. It is only a technicality, at best.

I now have another secret that I want to talk over with you at first chance. It concerns my new ranch foreman, Michael Bastrop. He has been with the ranch only a few months, but

From that point on, the writing was blotted out by the dark smear. Lee could only make out a few words here and there. "Impressed," "marriage," "disillusioned."

There was no signature. The writer had been interrupted, evidently, in the act of penning the closing line.

Lee knew that the grim discoloration had been made by blood. The blood of his mother. He looked up at Eagle. There was little chance the chief could read. Therefore he held such matters in awe and respect. In this case there probably was superstitious dread involved that had prevailed on the Comanche to preserve the letter.

Lee lifted out the photograph. It was coated with dust and soiled, but was still a remarkably clear print, made no doubt by one of the old, itinerant, wet-plate cameramen.

It was a posed picture of a beautiful, young, dark-eyed matron with a small boy on her lap, both in their best garb. Penned across the bottom of the picture was an inscription:

> *Dear Rose: As you can see, Juano is growing up.*
> *Margarita*

Eagle placed a gnarled finger on the picture of the child. "You," he said. "You. Wa-no-lo-pay."

Here was final proof. Lee knew beyond all doubt that he held in his hand a picture of himself with his mother. He was the son of John Calvin and the beautiful señorita who had been the heiress to Rancho Verde.

His mother must have been writing this letter when death had swept down on her as she sat at her desk. The "Rose" to whom she had been addressing the message could be none other than Clemmy's mother, who at that time had not yet married Clem O'Neil.

Memories that had been imbedded in the horrified mind of a child came to life, bleak and terrible. It was Eagle himself who had delivered the death blow when he led his warriors into the ranch house in broad daylight.

The haze of fury engulfed Lee again. Eagle snatched up the carbine to fight to the last, for he expected to be shot.

At that moment an unshaven man, wearing a grease-stained buckskin shirt and leather brush leggings, appeared in the opening and shouted, "Here he is, boys! Just like I said it would be from the reward posters. Put up your hands, Jackson! We've got you!"

At the intruder's shoulder were two more roughly garbed men. All had weapons in their hands. In the background Lee sighted a dun-colored pony.

He whirled, firing his six-shooter. The unshaven man touched off his rifle at the same moment. Neither bullet struck its intended target. Lee heard his opponent's slug smash through flesh back of him. His own shot missed.

He fired again, but the arrivals were all diving away from the entrance to the lodge, and the bullet had no target to find.

Eagle-in-the-Sky, blood flowing from his mouth, was sinking to his knees, clutching at his breast. He was trying to speak. Perhaps it was the death song he was attempting. He failed, for he pitched on his face on the lodge floor.

The bullet that had been meant for Lee had torn through his lungs. The medicine man's prophecy had been fulfilled: Eagle-in-the-Sky had died at Lee's feet.

The leader of the strangers was shouting orders, but his companions were yelling too, in confusion. Lee sent another bullet through the opening to discourage any attempt to enter.

The squaws had been using one area of the lodge as their sewing shop where they carried on the never-ending task of making garments and moccasins of buckskin. A knife lay among the homemade needles and awls.

Lee seized the knife, slashed a slit in the rear wall of the lodge, and leaped into the open. He was not sighted until he had traveled half a dozen strides. Then the reward hunters came howling in pursuit and began shooting.

He swerved, circling the lodge, keeping its bulk between himself and the trio. His strategy succeeded. He drew them away from the horses in front of the lodge. Both his roan and the Barb were rearing, terrified by the gunfire.

He reached the saddle of the roan as one of the

strangers came in sight. He fired and missed, but the shot served to drive its target back to hiding.

He grabbed the trailing reins of the roan. The knife was still in his left hand. He leaped into the saddle, leaned, and slashed the picket line the Barb was fighting.

He whirled the roan and hung on the far side of the saddle as he headed away. Indian fashion. Comanche style. But now that thought aroused no bitterness.

Bullets raged past. He swerved among the lodges to distract their aim. A slug struck the saddle horn, its force sending the roan off balance. It staggered to its knees. That probably saved the lives of both the horse and Lee, for the next slug stung the tip of the roan's ear. That bullet might have brained the animal had it been on its feet.

The injury goaded the roan to its feet and to frenzied speed. Looking back, Lee saw his pursuers running toward their horses. Their animals had been spooked by the uproar, and were rearing away from their owners.

In another direction, the Barb was running free, heading through the timber south of the village. The stallion was a part of the lilac shadows that were gathering in the thickets.

Lee rode west, away from where Kinky Bob and Clemmy would be waiting. He continued in that direction until darkness had come and he was sure he had shaken them off.

He still had the letter his mother had been writing when she had died, along with the photograph. He had thrust them inside his shirt when he had fled from the lodge.

CHAPTER FOURTEEN

He rode south until sure he had shaken off all chance they were still on his trail, then circled eastward. After some difficulty in the darkness he made his way back to where Clemmy and Kinky Bob waited.

Clemmy came running to his side as he slid from the saddle. "We thought—we were afraid—!" she babbled. "We heard shooting far away."

He kissed her. "I'm all right," he said. "I'll tell you about it while we're riding. Saddle up, Kink."

"Are they after us, Jack-Lee?"

"In a way, yes. But we're heading for home."

"Home?" Clemmy exclaimed.

"Punchbowl. That's our home. That's where we belong. Those hunters we spotted a day or two ago were smarter than I figured. They had sighted us, after all, and had guessed who we were. We seem to be pretty well advertised. They must have set up a blind trail to fool me into believing they had no interest in us, then circled back and followed us, waiting a chance to earn Mike Bastrop's offer of five thousand for me and a thousand for Kink. Dead."

After they were mounted and heading south he told them about the appearance of the hunters in Eagle's lodge and his escape.

"What did you learn from Eagle?" Clemmy demanded. "You found out something. Something good. You're different. You've changed."

"Eagle gave me a photograph and an unfinished letter in exchange for the Barb," he said. "My mother was writing the letter years ago to your mother."

"To my mother?"

"It was being written before you were born, before your mother had married Clem O'Neil," Lee said.

"They—they knew each other?"

"They must have been very close friends. And why not? They were of about the same age. Both had been raised in the Punchbowl. In fact, it was addressed to her dearest friend, Rose."

He repeated the gist of the letter. "My mother must have been writing it when Eagle burst into the room to kill her," he said. "She must have managed to get a gun, and shot him. He was scarred for life. He killed her, and he and his Comanches took me with them when they left. He hated that scar and made me pay for it. He hated me."

"Nevertheless, you can't really think of going back to Punchbowl," Clemmy protested. "Nothing's really changed. They'd never believe you, or that the letter isn't a fake. And they'd still charge you with killing Uncle Tice, no doubt."

"I want to ask a few questions of a certain party in Punchbowl," Lee said. "Judge Clebe."

"But—"

"Let's think back to the night Bill Tice was killed," Lee said. "Let's go over everything you remember, step by step. We know that the killing was done with that .32 you still have. You said you ran out of your room to follow Merl when he set out to chase me. You're sure you didn't have the gun with you?"

"Yes. I'm sure of that. I must have tossed it on the sofa. It was there when I came back."

"On the sofa?"

"Yes. I'm almost positive it was. I was excited, of course, by the shooting. The room reeked of powder smoke. I panicked when I heard Merl screeching that Uncle Tice was dead and that I had killed him. I took the gun with me when I ran and jumped on Major Bastrop's horse."

"Could anyone have been in your room and fired the shots through the window before you came back?"

"I suppose so. I don't know where the others were. It probably could have been most anyone."

"But Clebe and Mike Bastrop were the only ones around," Lee said. "Merl was chasing me."

They let the horses settle down to a long gait that they could keep up indefinitely. "I've got a hunch we can't let grass grow under us," Lee said. "Those three men will still try to cash in. And they know where the money will come from. Mike Bastrop. They'll try to get to Bastrop as fast as possible. And I think Mike Bastrop will know why we went to Eagle-in-the-Sky. He'll know that I'm sure now that I am John and Margarita Calvin's son."

He added, "That means I might be the legal owner of Rancho Verde."

"Isn't it the law that a husband inherits all of a wife's property?" Clemmy said dubiously.

"That's true. But what about the will my mother mentioned? Your mother was named in it, but the will that was filed seemed to have left everything to Mike Bastrop."

"I see what you mean. A fake will. But that means—"

"Sure," Lee said. "That means Judge Clebe was in on it. And Bill Tice. They were witnesses to the real will."

"Oh, my goodness!" Clemmy breathed excitedly. Then her animation faded. "But proving it is something else. What chance would you have against Amos Clebe and Major Bastrop? They've got all the advantage, including money."

"If Clebe forged my mother's will, he might have pulled a few other tricks," Lee said. "Such as faking a marriage license."

"You mean you don't believe your mother was married to Major Bastrop?"

"I don't know what to think. There are a few words I could make out in the stained part of the letter that seemed to be referring to Bastrop. One was 'marriage.' Another was 'impressed.' That might mean she was secretly married to him. But it might not. There was another word, 'disillusioned.' It's my guess that what she was saying was that she had been impressed by Bastrop when she first hired him as foreman at the ranch, that he had proposed marriage and that she had decided to fire him, being disillusioned with him."

"Of course," Clemmy breathed. "A lot of things are beginning to add up."

"Speaking of wills," Lee said. "Did you ever see the one your mother made out?"

"No. I was only a child at the time, of course. All I know is that they say Mother left nothing, and that Uncle Tice, as my only kin, was appointed my guardian by the court."

"The court. By Judge Clebe, in other words. That

means that, as guardian, Bill Tice had control of any money your mother actually might have left you. I've heard that Rose O'Neil was paid pretty high as a singer. What became of it?"

"I've always believed in my heart that Uncle Tice cheated me out of a lot of money," Clemmy sighed. "But by the time I was grown up enough to realize it, it was too late."

"He likely split it with Judge Clebe," Lee said. "They figured that if that sort of a scheme had worked when my mother died, it was worth trying again. They saw to it that your mother's name was maligned in order to keep you from asking questions, and to make it unpopular for anyone to take your side against them. They didn't dare do away with you. They only tried to break your spirit so you'd never cause trouble for them."

"The same way they tried to force you to break your neck riding bad horses and taking the worst of it on the trail," she said.

"We've *got* to talk to Amos Clebe," Lee said. "Alone!"

He was remembering the bodyguards Kink had said were looking after Judge Clebe's safety. He guessed that Clemmy and Kink were thinking of them also.

Darkness of the third day of their long ride came before they sighted the lights of Punchbowl ahead. They were mounted on their third relay of horses. They had seized fresh mounts at isolated ranches along the way and had been forced to take them at gun point, for they had been recognized by the owners of the animals they had commandeered.

"Send the bill to Rancho Verde," Lee had told them. "If I'm alive, it will be paid. Forget about earning the rewards Mike Bastrop has placed on our heads. Bastrop might not be in a position to pay blood money."

Lee felt certain the hunters who had tried to earn the bounty would be heading for Punchbowl to notify Mike Bastrop of their discovery, hoping to salvage at least a part of the reward for their pains. These men would have an advantage in the race to Punchbowl. Their horses were comparatively fresh at the start. Furthermore, they could ride openly on the trails, rather than the devious paths Lee and his companions were forced to take at times to avoid settlements where they might be recognized and halted.

The three of them had lost more weight from bodies that had already been thinned by hardships. Now, with the lights of Punchbowl ahead, they had the lean aspect of wolves. Their eyes were sunken in faces burned by sun and wind. Their clothes flapped on them in the wind.

They skirted the town and dismounted in the brush along Punchbowl Creek near the spot where Clemmy had waited the night Lee had gone into the town for supplies.

The hot spell had ended. A chill wind, whispering of the coming of winter, droned through the brush and rattled store signs and loose clapboards in the town. Clemmy clasped her arms across her breast and moaned with cold and weariness.

To gain information that Lee wanted, Kink left them and headed off into the darkness on foot, hoping to get in touch with his friend Celia. Clemmy huddled against Lee and they settled down to wait. She fell asleep, clinging to him, still moaning in her slumber.

The wait went on, and became an ordeal. "If anything goes wrong," Lee had told Kinky Bob, "just shoot in the air. I'll come in. Don't try any fool thing like leading them away from us. And don't shoot anybody. If there's anything like that to be done, I'm the one to do it."

Lee did not move, not wanting to awaken Clemmy. He watched the swing of the Big Dipper, using a dead tree as a guide, in order to keep track of time.

He judged that the hour was past eleven and he had almost convinced himself that he should wait no longer, but must enter the town in search of the big man, when Kink came back out of the darkness.

"I had to lay low quite a spell afore I had a chance to crawl in an' talk to Celia," Kink explained. "She's still cook an' housekeeper for de Judge. She live dar in a little room back o' de kitchen. She wants to quit, but she skeered to."

"Scared?"

"Judge Clebe, he skeered too. He keep dem bodyguards o' his mighty close to de house at nights. Dat's why I had to wait 'til I was sure I could wriggle to de back door an' git Celia to let me in."

"You were in the house? In Clebe's house?"

"Inside, safest place to be. One o' dem slingers always on de watch an' prowls around de outside o' the house every once in a while all night long. Celia know somebody goin' to git killed sooner or later. She mighty worked up, I tell you."

"Does she happen to know just who the Judge is afraid might come for him?"

"Celia don't know dat. She say de Judge is drinkin' harder'n ever, an' is mighty, mighty nervous. Jumps if'n a door slams. Two o' dem gunmen go with him to court every day, an' stay with him every step."

"What about Mike Bastrop?"

"Celia say she ain't seen hide nor hair o' him in town since somebody put dat bullet in his arm."

"And Merl and Gabe Tice?"

"She say de Judge is 'special keerful to steer clear o' dem two scamps. Dey in town most o' de time, drinkin' an' playin' cards. Dey're in Punchbowl right now. Least ways, Celia saw dem early dis evenin' when she was shoppin' at Sim Quarles' store."

"Did you remember to ask her if the Judge keeps any papers in the house, and if so, where?"

"If he's got any in the house, Celia say they're in a big iron safe dat's built into the wall back of a dresser in de Judge's bedroom. She say de Judge got powerful mad at her one time when she moved de dresser so she could sweep de carpet, an' saw de safe. Dat was de first time she knew it was there."

Lee shook hands with the big man. "I know you took your life in your hands to go into that house," he said. "That's another thing I'll always remember."

He added, "We'll leave the horses here. Mark the place well so that you can find it in a hurry if need be."

The three of them moved through the back areas of the town. The only activity in Sumner Street at this hour was in the gambling houses, and even there the patronage evidently was very light.

They made their way to Amos Clebe's residence, which had been built away from any neighbors for the sake of seclusion. It was a pretentious structure with two stories and a high-gabled attic, all adorned with fretwork and turrets. A white picket fence enclosed the tree-shaded grounds. Leaves flew in the brisk wind.

Kinky Bob led the way to the rear. They scaled the fence, Lee lifting Clemmy over the barrier. Heeding

Kink's warning for silence, they crawled on hands and knees, a few feet at a time.

They were still a dozen yards from the house when they heard footsteps on the veranda at the front. They flattened to the ground, and watched the glow of a masked bull's-eye lantern that marked the location of someone who had emerged from the front door of the mansion.

It was an inspection trip. The blind on the lantern was snapped open and shut, with the beam of light darting briefly over windows and doors. Once the light passed almost over their huddled bodies, but the sentry moved on without discovering them.

Lee detected the odor of cheap whisky and rank pipe tobacco. The bodyguard, evidently bored with his lonely duty, was taking steps to make the task more bearable.

A heavier rush of wind roared through the trees. Lee arose and ran, his six-shooter lifted above his head. The wind helped cover the sound of his footfalls. His quarry heard him at the last moment and turned. But too late. Lee slashed the muzzle of the weapon across the man's neck. The blow numbed nerves. The only sound was a gasp. He caught the sagging weight of his victim and lowered him to the ground.

Clemmy rushed up and picked up the lantern which had fallen to the ground. She snapped the slide closed, masking it, and waited a moment until the flickering of the flame steadied.

Kink joined them. They crouched, waiting and listening. No sign of alarm came from the house. Lee and Kink bound the dazed man's ankles and wrists and gagged him with sleeves torn from his own shirt.

Lee took the lantern from Clemmy and led the way to the front of the house. No light showed inside. He mounted the veranda and tiptoed to the dark door. It stood ajar. The sentry evidently had intended to return by this route after circling the house.

Lee pushed open the door and unmasked the lantern. The beam of light probed a richly carpeted entry hall. To the left, a wide arched opening led to an ornately furnished parlor. A carpeted stairway mounted to rooms above. At the rear of the hall an open door revealed a sizable kitchen.

Another door stood at the right, midway down the hall.

The snoring of sleepers was audible. Lee moved down the hall, Kink at his heels, while Clemmy waited. Lee stepped into the side room, flashing the beam of light around.

A man in his underwear was sprawled on a bed, asleep. A second sleeper lay on a cot. Another cot stood in a corner, evidently the bed of the man they had left bound outside.

Lee gave Kink the lantern. "Keep 'em blinded," he whispered.

He moved to the bed, seized the sleeper by the hair, and shook him. He jammed a boot into the ribs of the man on the cot.

Both men tried to leap to their feet, befuddled. Their instinct was to reach for weapons, but their gunbelts had been draped over chairs out of reach. Lee pushed them back onto their beds.

"Lie face down!" he whispered. "And don't say a word unless you want a broken skull. Not a word!"

He thrust his six-shooter into the beam of light so they could see it.

"Your partner outside has been taken care of," he added. "You'll get no help from him. Don't try to earn your pay by asking for a bullet. It isn't worth it. You can believe that. Stretch out face-down and put your hands back of you. We're not interested in you two leppies. We're after bigger game."

They obeyed. "You must be thet damned Comanch' what punched the ticket o' that cattleman at BT," one of them grunted.

Lee rapped him sharply on the head with the muzzle of the pistol. "That will only raise a lump," he said. "One more peep out of you, and you'll wake up with the devil poking a pitchfork into you."

The man went rigidly silent. Neither he nor his companion offered opposition as Kink lashed their ankles to their wrists behind their backs and gagged them with strips from the bedding.

Lee saw a second bull's-eye lantern on the shelf. He found it in working order and lighted it, then handed it to Clemmy. "Keep watch on these two and anything that might come up outside," he said.

He and Kink mounted the stairs to the second floor. Their feet made no sound on the carpet. The beam of the lantern picked out the doors of four bedrooms. A narrower stair led to what evidently were quarters in the turrets and gables above.

"Ain't nobody up dar," Kink murmured.

Three of the bedrooms were unlocked and unoccupied. The door of the fourth room was locked when Lee cautiously tested the knob. He looked at Kink, who nodded.

Kink backed away a pace and crashed his weight against the door. The lock was torn from its moorings. Kink plunged into the room, falling to his knees. Lee nearly toppled over him, but steadied himself, darting the beam of the lamp around.

The light settled on Judge Amos Clebe in a nightshift. The Judge was sitting, startled, in bed and swinging a cocked Colt .44 back and forth, ready to shoot.

He was blinded by the light. Before he could make up his mind whether to fire or not, Lee came out of the shadows and clamped a hand over the gun, jamming the hammer with his thumb so that it could not fall.

He twisted the weapon from the Judge's grasp. "My God, Mike!" Amos Clebe croaked. "Give me a chance! Let's talk this over sanely. We can come to an understanding."

"What sort of an understanding?" Lee demanded.

Amos Clebe blinked, trying to avoid the beam of light in order to make out Lee's shadowy face. "It *is* you, isn't it Mike?" he asked shrilly.

"Guess again," Lee said.

Amos Clebe ran a tongue over dry lips. "It's not—not—"

"Yes," Lee said. "You might be better off if it had been Mike Bastrop. But, unlucky for you, it's John Calvin. John Lopez Calvin, Margarita Calvin's son. Otherwise known as Lee Jackson."

CHAPTER FIFTEEN

The shock of it silenced Amos Clebe for a space. Then he tried to bluster it out. "You must be insane. Margarita Calvin's child was killed by Comanches years ago and you know it."

"It's no use," Lee said. "I've learned about my mother's will. The real will, not the fake one you drew up after her death, which left everything to Mike Bastrop."

"How—?" Clebe began to mumble. Then he realized his mistake, and tried to cover it up. "I'd say you are really out of your mind, or that you think you can attempt blackmail."

"You know a lot about blackmail, I imagine, Judge," Lee said. "My mother was never married to Mike Bastrop, was she, secretly or otherwise? That's another lie you manufactured."

"What kind of foolishness—?" Clebe began. He had been deluded by the level tone of Lee's voice.

Lee slapped him. The blow sent the man back onto his pillow, gasping.

"You drew up a fake marriage license and dated it two months before her death," he said. "You and Bastrop saw your chance to own Rancho Verde. You had to take Bill Tice in on the deal because he knew about the real will."

Lee was pretending an assurance he did not really possess. He was guessing and believed he was right, but he still had no actual proof. But his manner was more convincing than he realized.

Amos Clebe made a last desperate attempt to brazen it out, but the blow had driven terror through him and it showed in his voice. "I—I don't know what you're talking about."

"Was it Bastrop who murdered Bill Tice that night?" Lee demanded. "Was it Bastrop who used Clemmy O'Neil's .32, firing from the window of her room, then left the gun in the room so that the murder would be put against her? Or against me?"

Amos Clebe's bearded face was suddenly gray and haggard. He tried to answer, failed.

"Or was it you who murdered Bill Tice?" Lee went on. "It was one or the other of you."

"No!" Clebe gasped. "No! I didn't do it! I was at the front of the house. I was drunk, but not drunk enough to—"

"To know murder when you saw it," Lee said. "Then you *did* see it. And so did I. So it *was* the Major who killed him."

Clebe could not answer. But the admission was written on his face.

"You were afraid you'd be the next to go," Lee said. "You and Bill Tice had milked Bastrop for years, forcing him to share the profits from Rancho Verde. That's why the Tices blossomed out after living so long on hard scrabble, and that's why Bill Tice became a partner in Rancho Verde. And that's why you've been able to live like a rich man. Likely you two began hogging more than your share of the money and Bastrop decided to get rid of both of you."

He dragged Amos Clebe from the bed, hurled him on the floor, and jammed a boot heel against his throat. "You figured you would have to kill Mike Bastrop before he killed you like he did Bill Tice. Bastrop had decided to quit being a front man for you leeches and was going for all the profits from Rancho Verde. You saw a chance to dust him in the back that night you spotted his horse in front of the Silver Bell. You hurried home to get a gun, came back, and waited until he came out of the Bell. I interfered, or you'd have put him out of the way for keeps. And you'd have seen to it that I got the blame. It was just by luck that I happened to be right there at the right time. Or was it the wrong time?"

He flashed the beam of light around the room and halted it on a big walnut dresser. "Move it, Kink," he said.

Kink shoved the dresser aside, revealing the door of an iron combination safe, set in the wall.

Lee grasped Amos Clebe by his wiry gray beard and dragged him to the safe. "Open it!" he ordered.

Clebe moaned again, looking up at him. "Open it!" Lee repeated. "You might get off with only a jolt in prison, if you tell the truth. After all, you haven't murdered anybody—yet."

Amos Clebe got to his knees and began fumbling with the knob. Lee rapped his hands with the muzzle of the pistol. "Quit stalling. Open it the easy way, or with some fingers busted. It's your choice."

He jammed Clebe's nose roughly against the metal surface of the safe. "No, please! Please!" Clebe moaned. "I'll open it."

The man manipulated the knob, his hands trembling. The door of the safe swung open. Its compartments were well filled with filed documents. One section was stuffed with packets of greenbacks.

"You were making sure you wouldn't be exactly broke if you had to pull out in a hurry," Lee commented.

He added, "You know what I want. My mother's will. The real one. I know it's here. You never destroyed your copy of it. Nor did Bill Tice, I'm sure. Both of you needed the copies as a club to keep Mike Bastrop in line. I want Rose O'Neil's will also. Don't make me go through all those papers to find them."

Clebe thought of trying to brave it out, but didn't have the fortitude. With shaking fingers he delved through a packet of papers that he drew from an inner, locked drawer in the safe. Presently he handed one over.

Lee did not attempt to read it. He was sure it was the will his mother had made out. "How about Rose O'Neil's will?" he demanded.

"I—I destroyed it years ago," Clebe admitted.

"How much money did she leave to Clemmy?" Lee asked.

"Why—why, nothing. She—"

Lee jammed the pistol muzzle jarringly into the Judge's teeth. "How much?"

"Please don't hurt me!" Clebe chattered. "It was about—about sixty thousand dollars."

Lee gave Kink a tight grin. "You can tell Clemmy that she'll likely soon be the owner of BT. It should be about worth what the Tices owe her after all these years."

At that moment, Clemmy, from below, uttered a sound of warning. Kink snapped the hood closed on the lantern.

She came silently up the stairs in the darkness. "There's someone outside," she murmured.

Lee jammed the bore of his six-shooter hard into Amos Clebe's back. "Don't make a sound!" he warned. "Not a sound!"

They waited. Utter silence held for a time. Lee was beginning to believe Clemmy had been mistaken.

Then a voice spoke guardedly in the darkness at the front of the house. "Amos! Amos! Wake up! It's Mike! Call off your bodyguards. It's Mike. I want to talk to you! Wake up!"

Lee prodded Amos Clebe again. "Answer him!" he breathed. "Ask what he wants."

Clebe croaked something, but it was unintelligible even to Lee. However, it fitted the situation, for it could have been the voice of a man suddenly awakened from sound sleep.

"We've got to have a talk, Amos," Bastrop repeated. "It's important. Something's come up. Promise me I won't be shot. I'll come onto the porch."

"Talk?" Clebe called hoarsely. His curiosity was genuine. "What about?"

"Speak to your men," Bastrop insisted. "Are they in the house? If so, I don't want them to open up on me. I'm not armed. My gun is still on the saddle."

"Tell him to come onto the porch," Lee murmured.

"No, no!" Clebe groaned. "He's lying. He's come here to kill me. He'll be armed."

"I'll see to it that you come out of it, still breathing," Lee said. "I need you alive, Judge. I need you very much."

Mike Bastrop raised another impatient demand. "Amos! Let me in!"

"Answer," Lee ordered. "Say, 'I'm coming down to meet you at the door, Mike.' "

Amos Clebe gained a measure of steadiness and repeated the words. He had accepted the fact that his only hope was to obey.

Lee prodded him to his feet. "I'm going down with you," he murmured.

Carrying the masked lantern, he prodded his prisoner down the stairs ahead of him.

Clemmy had closed the front door after their entrance. Lee heard the footsteps of Mike Bastrop as he mounted the steps and crossed the veranda. Bastrop was standing at the door, waiting.

Lee unmasked the lantern, letting the circle of light fall on the door. He pushed Clebe toward the portal. "Open it!" he breathed.

Amos Clebe feared to open the door. He was suddenly frozen by terror. Lee reached past him, freed the latch, and let the door swing inward.

Mike Bastrop stood, blinded by the lantern. He raised an arm to shield his eyes from the light. He wore no weapon—in sight at least. Evidently he had recovered from the arm wound that Amos Clebe had inflicted, for there was no sign of a bandage.

"I can't see a damned thing, Amos," he complained. "Turn that light off. I'm coming in. There's the devil to pay."

Lee drew Clebe back from the door. Mike Bastrop took that as an invitation to enter and stepped in.

"I'm afraid a certain party knows too much," Bastrop said. "He's talked to a Comanche chief. You can guess who it was, I imagine."

Lee poked Clebe into answering. "I can guess."

"A man showed up at Casa Bonita tonight," Bastrop said. "He had two more men with him. They likely make their living with a running iron and stealing horses, but I think he told the truth this time. He and his pals sighted a white man, a black man, and a girl dressed as a boy, way up north on the Comanche reserve. They followed one of them into Eagle's village and tried to grab him, for he was Lee Jackson. Jackson got away. This man and his pals killed a few horses getting to Rancho Verde to tell me they're sure Jackson was heading toward Punchbowl with his two friends."

He waited for Clebe to speak. He became impatient, again trying to shield his eyes from the light. "Stop blinding me, Amos," he snarled. "If you've got a gun on me, put it away. We've got to pull together. If young Calvin shows up here, you know what that will mean."

Clebe's continued silence sparked a warning in Bastrop's mind.

"Is someone there with you, Amos?" he demanded.

Lee spoke. "Yes. It's young Calvin. I got to the Punchbowl ahead of the bounty hunters, Major. By the way, were you ever really in the Confederate Army? Everything else about you is wrong."

Mike Bastrop had lied. He *was* armed. His reaction was very fast. A six-shooter appeared in his hand. He had been carrying it thrust in the rear of his belt.

He fired twice. But he missed, for coming at him was the bull's-eye lantern. Lee had hurled the lantern the instant Bastrop moved. At the same time he fell aside, jerking Amos Clebe with him.

The lantern struck Bastrop in the face. The man fired a third shot, but this slug went wild as had the first two.

Lee dived forward, bowling Bastrop off his feet. He knew that Bastrop would attempt to turn the gun on him. He brought his head up against Bastrop's chin, and teeth shattered. He swung an arm and it batted Bastrop's gun aside as it exploded a fourth time. He drove a fist deep into Bastrop's stomach and brought a knee into the groin.

He felt Bastrop sag, then go down with bubbling sounds of agony. Lee yanked the gun from the man's hand. He crouched, listening in case others were out there in the darkness. But there was no sound.

Bastrop had come here alone. He had not wanted witnesses, for Lee surmised that he had come here to commit another murder. He had wanted to make sure that Amos Clebe would never live to face Lee.

"*Lee?*" Clemmy screamed from the head of the stairs. "Lee?"

"I'm all right," Lee said. "How about you and Kink?"

The beam of the second lantern lightened the stairs as Kink unmasked it. "Keno," Kink said. "But one o' dem slugs shore came mighty close to givin' ol' Kink a part in his hair."

They joined Lee. Lee searched Mike Bastrop for additional weapons, but found only a sleeve knife. He swung the light on Amos Clebe. The pudgy Judge sat numbly against the wall. At first Lee believed he had been hit by a bullet. But Clebe's injury was despair. He was a collapsed balloon. Flaccid, beset by self-pity.

Bastrop began to recover. He cursed Clebe with savage anger and contempt. "You gutless, yellow-livered thief," he panted. "You thought up this whole scheme, but I always knew you'd be the first to turn yellow if pressure was put on you."

He glared into the lantern beam. "I'm not going to let this hypocrite nor Bill Tice's two whelps put all of this on me. They're in it too."

"Merl and Gabe know about how my mother's will was faked?" Lee asked.

"They found it out a long time ago," Bastrop said. "Bill Tice was fool enough to keep a copy of the real will and those two found it when they were going through things that wasn't any of their business."

"We'll ask them if they still have that copy," Lee said.

"Ask them? We?"

"Get on your feet," Lee said. "You too, Judge. We're going for a walk. The Tices were in town earlier in the evening. Maybe they still are. If they heard the shooting, they might even be wondering if it meant that you had taken care of Judge Clebe like you took care of their father."

"It was this doughbelly who calls himself a judge who shot Bill Tice in the back," Bastrop snapped.

"Oh, no you don't, Bastrop!" Clebe panted. "You did it."

They began raving at each other. Lee put an end to it by yanking both of them to their feet.

"Keep your gun in the Judge's back, Kink," he said. "If he tries to run, shoot him. I'll do the same for Bastrop."

"You ain't really aimin' on lookin' up dem Tice boys?" Kink asked dubiously.

"I don't intend to let them get away," Lee said. "They'll be long gone for Mexico if they get spooked."

He sent Bastrop ahead of him with a shove. "Get used to it," he said. "Prison guards want action when they give an order. So does the hangman."

The stiff wind evidently had carried the sound of the gunshots away from the heart of Punchbowl, for Sumner Street was deserted when they turned into it from a side street. Dust blew and signs creaked. Loose sheet-iron banged on a roof.

It was past midnight and the Silver Bell was the only saloon still open. The two flashy California sorrels that Gabe and Merl Tice preferred as saddle mounts stood at the rail in front of the gambling house.

Mike Bastrop halted. "Don't make me walk in there," he said.

"Why not?"

"They'll come up shooting. At least give me a gun to defend myself."

"What you mean is that they know you murdered their father, but didn't give a hoot as long as it gave them more money to spend. Now, you figure that when they see you and Clebe with me they'll know that all four of you have reached the end of the rope, and they'll try to shoot you to keep you from doing any more talking. A fine handful of cold-blooded sharks."

Bastrop grasped at a new straw. "You've got it wrong," he exclaimed. "They're the ones who killed Bill Tice. Bill would never give them all the money they wanted for their drinking and gambling, so—"

"That's it!" Amos Clebe blurted, pouncing on this possible avenue of safety. "That's the way it was. Gabe is the one, most likely. He's capable of it. He always despised his father."

"I'll tell them what you said," Lee said. "Especially Gabe."

He sent Bastrop through the swing doors with a push that sprawled him on the floor inside. He caught Clebe by the throat and shoved him into the gambling house where he fell over Bastrop.

Merl and Gabe Tice had been playing poker at a rear table with two cowboys whom Lee recognized as being from the Fiddleback outfit north of the Armadillo Hills. The Fiddleback men could be expected to remain neutral.

The only other patron of the place at this late hour was Sheriff Fred Mack who was standing at the bar, drinking a nightcap.

The Tice brothers had leaped to their feet. Lee stepped in, his six-shooter in his hand. Clemmy and Kink started to follow him. "Stay back," he said. "Kink, keep out of this!"

He addressed the sheriff. "Glad you're here, sheriff. I'll turn these people over to you. All of them are mixed up in stealing Rancho Verde, in blackmail, embezzlement, and forgery. Not to mention murder."

He looked at the Tice brothers. "The murder of Bill Tice. Bastrop and Judge Clebe say one or the other of you killed your father so as to get for yourselves all the profits from BT and from blackmailing Mike Bastrop."

"What's that?" Merl yelled. "Why, the dirty liars! It was one o' them that—"

"Shut *up!*" his brother growled.

"They said you probably were the one, Gabe," Lee said. "Get enough of them against you and you'll swing whether you did it or not. Sheriff, I'm asking you to arrest these men. I've got documents and witnesses that will convict them all. In addition to stealing Rancho Verde, they helped defraud Clemmy O'Neil of a lot of money."

Gabe Tice went for his gun. Lee fired, but not to kill. The bullet struck Gabe high on the right arm, shattering his shoulder. Blood spurted. The impact drove him sprawling back on the poker table. The two Fiddleback riders were diving to cover. Gabe's half-drawn gun fell from his hand.

Merl, always slower-witted, was also slower on the draw.

"Hold it, Merl!" Lee warned. "I just fixed it so that Gabe never will be able to swing a quirt on a horse, most likely, let alone on a man. I'd mighty like to do the same favor for you. And I will if you try to pull that gun."

Merl let his hands rise into the air. "We didn't do it!" he almost screamed. "We didn't kill our own Paw. You did it, you Comanch' devil, an' you know it."

"You're a liar, Merl," Lee said. "You know who killed your Paw. And my name is John Lopez Calvin, not Comanch'. I never took it kindly when they called me that in the past. I'm going to be still more touchy about it in the future."

He added, "They're all yours, sheriff."

Fred Mack stood confused for a time. Then he acted. "We'll go a little deeper into this at the jail," he said. "One of you Fiddleback boys will serve as deputy to help me lead these men to my office. The other better go an' fetch Doc Peters to fix up Gabe's arm."

Dawn was near when Lee and Clemmy emerged from the door of the jail, followed by Kink. Lamplight still burned in the jail office where Fred Mack was at his desk, pen in hand, writing his report. Mike Bastrop, Amos Clebe, and the Tices were locked up in cells.

It had taken hours of questioning, of sifting the truth from the evasions, denials, and attempts of the four to blame each other.

But there was no doubt that Mike Bastrop had slain Bill Tice and would go on trial for his life, sooner or later. Amos Clebe would face a long list of charges and the Tice brothers stood to serve time also for abetting the fraud.

The three of them stood soberly in the darkness of deserted Sumner Street. Their worn clothes flapped about their thin bodies in the wind. The Silver Bell had closed. The town was dismal and lonely.

Clemmy was shaking. Once again Lee lifted her in his arms and carried her.

"Where are we going?" she asked exhaustedly.

"To Rancho Verde," he said. "To Spirit Lake. To everywhere. To the world. To everything we've always wanted to see and do. Together."

"We goin' to walk to all dem places?" Kink wailed. "My laigs are mighty, mighty tired, Jack-Lee."

All three of them suddenly began to laugh. They stood there together in the lonely street of Punchbowl, laughing wildly.